L.E. EL

A YULEAN SISTER'S GUIDE TO GETTING

MARRIED

COVER ART: PHANTOM DAME

DEVELOPMENTAL EDITING: LYONNE RILEY

COPY EDITING AND PROOFREADING: ALEXA THOMAS AT THE FICTION FIX

BETA READERS: ELAINE DANIELS AND LIZZIE STRONG

FORMATTED BY MALDO DESIGNS

TO MY MOTHER.

THANK YOU FOR ALWAYS
SUPPORTING MY DREAMS.

LAYRUNE

◉ KALOPIEA

THVETHARION

ASHMORE

VALCOR

MERTIS

◉ SOBURY

QUVILL

◉ MORADAN

CONTENT WARNING

This is a generally cozy book, but it does come with some content warnings, so please review them carefully. If you have any questions about them, please feel free to email me at lexie@morallygrayreads.com

Content warnings:

Somnophilia
Bondage
breeding (w/o pregnancy)
Voyeurism
cock warming
Mentions of substance abuse
Side character with substance abuse history
BDSM elements
Murder
Violence and gore
Slight themes of misogyny (not from main characters)
Sexually explicit scenes
Mention of abuse attempt (not by main characters)
Choking/light breath play
Brief discussion of torture (no specifics described)

Enjoy ;)

CHAPTER ONE

ZARIOS

MY HOOF TAPPED THE floor of the carriage, impatience rolling through me. I knew Kiaza must be getting sick of the sound, but she was too kind to say anything. I looked out the window over the rolling hills covered in trees. Stalks of long grass rose from the ground, sitting against the blue sky and forest in the distance. Though it was beautiful, I didn't have the brain space to appreciate it.

Since becoming Grand Clarak four short years ago, it had been one thing after another. Not only was I at constant odds with the other Claraks on reform, but I was also battling a nasty group of thieves attacking our foreign traders. It started a few months back. They left almost everyone dead, with only a few survivors. They attacked a caravan going to Arnethian in the south, and another in Nasor to the East, both within a day of each other. It would be impossible to get between those two places in a day, even on horseback.

And to top it all off, because of the attacks, Peradona had stopped their shipment of magestones. Magestones were powerful, used as conduits for magic to keep fires lit longer or water running hot without the need to boil. They were essential to our blacksmiths and to keep our villages running. Most come from Nordin, the mountain country where ice dragons lived, but they weren't interested in trading with Valcor. Luckily, Peradona had their own smaller mining operation and were more than happy to trade with us—they even agreed to send already charged stones. Valcor had very few magic users, certainly not enough to charge all the stones we required.

So now, I was headed to Peradona to request the shipment of magestones once more. I wasn't quite sure how I would convince them they'd be safe yet, but I would figure it out.

"We're almost there, sire," Kiaza said across from me. She hardly looked up from her notebook, shoving her glasses back up her face. She was my assistant, and the best one at that. Without her, I probably wouldn't have made it to this meeting.

I looked back out the window and realized she was right. Gone were the vast fields, replaced with tight pastel buildings and bustling streets. "Good," I said, trying to stretch my legs as well as I could in this tight carriage. "I can't wait to get out of this thing. I don't know why I couldn't just ride my horse."

"You know how humans feel about appearances. We need to stay in their good graces." I groaned. Though I didn't like it, she was right. We needed them.

The carriage came around a bend and then to a halt. I looked up at a large building. Though we had castles, they looked nothing like this. The entire thing was white, with large spires and a grand staircase that led to a giant entrance. The grounds were perfectly manicured, topiaries lining the entire drive.

My Head of Guard Damyr came around and opened the door. We had been best friends since we were calves, alongside Naram, who was currently the Clarak of Mertis. I knew Damyr was the only one I wanted as my Head of Guard when I became Grand Clarak.

"Time to wake up," Damyr said jokingly.

"As if I could have slept in this rickety thing." That was a lie, the carriage was a perfectly smooth ride, but it was still cramped, and I would have much preferred riding myself.

I stepped out into the mid-day sun. The large doors opened, and a few guards came out, joined by servants. Behind them stood Yvon and Elsbeth Yulean, queens of this land. Yvon had long dark hair tied back in a simple braid. She wore a deep green dress and had sharp, observant eyes. Elsbeth seemed like her direct opposite. She had a glowing smile, with rounded cheeks and curly blonde locks. Though she looked much kinder, I was sure she was just as sharp.

They came down the steps to greet us as the servants grabbed our bags. "King Zarios," Elsbeth greeted with a slight bow. "Welcome. Thank you for coming so soon."

"Thank you for hosting," I said. "We're grateful for your hospitality."

"Of course," Yvon said, her voice a bit of a lower register. "We thought you may want to rest a bit before things got too formal, but we did want to see if you could quickly meet to begin discussions."

"No problem," I said. I wanted to leave here as soon as possible, so the quicker we reached an agreement, the better.

"I'll stay with the luggage and meet you in our rooms," Damyr said.

I gave him a nod, and Kiaza and I followed them inside. The floors were all marble tile, a carpeted runner along the floor. I wasn't sure if that was always there or placed recently so our hooves didn't click so loudly, but either way, I was grateful for it. There were white pillars scattered across the space, with a massive chandelier overhead beneath a glass ceiling. The sun beat down through it, casting small rainbows all over the space. Two grand staircases ran up the sides in front of us with a balcony above. I could see at least five floors going up from the bottom. With a quick glance overhead, I could see guards posted on each one, and took note of all of their positions.

Always get a feel for your surroundings, my father's voice echoed in my head. *It's one of the most important things, know your enemy.* Though I didn't consider Peradona an enemy for now, it was still sound advice.

We were led down the hall, past the staircase and towards what looked like offices. Once we reached the back, Yvon opened a door into a large conference room, a rounded table in the middle and a board to the front.

Kiaza and I took our seats on one side, with Yvon and Elsbeth on the other. Guards stood in two opposite corners of the room.

There was a knock on the door, and in walked a woman with brown hair tied back in a tight bun, a dragon behind her. I was slightly shocked to see him. Though Peradona was one of the most diverse kingdoms, it was considered human lands. Dragons tended to stick to their mountains. He stood in the unoccupied corner, closest to where the new woman sat.

"I hope you don't mind," Elsbeth said. "This is our daughter, Sybil. She's next in line for the throne, and we've looped her in on the situation."

That's fine," I said. "Nice to meet you."

She bowed slightly. "You as well."

I didn't return the gesture. In Valcor, you only bowed to admit defeat or to someone who ranked above you. As Grand Clarak, I bowed to no one. None of them seemed surprised, however, so I'm sure Kiaza filled them in before we arrived.

Another moment later, tea was brought in and poured. Once it was only us left in the room, the true discussion started.

"We have yet to receive the shipment of magestones," I said. "They are extremely important to our nation, and I wanted to see for myself if any changes needed to be made to our agreement."

"No changes," Yvon said. "We were curious ourselves. Almost every shipment that has gone out in the last few months has resulted in some kind of attack."

I kept my face neutral, but this was my worry. "Yes, we've had an unusually large number of thieves in the area, but we've put more guards on the road and are tracking them down."

While what I said was true, I didn't let on how far we truly were from making an arrest. It was just such a strange case, and every trail seemed to go cold.

"When do you expect to have this situation under control?" Yvon asked.

"Soon. That path is also secret to anyone outside of nobility, so it should be safe."

A look passed between the three of them, speaking without the direct need to use words. I had become that close with Damyr and Naram. All it took was a glance, and I knew exactly what the other was thinking.

"We will get you set up for the night," Elsbeth said, effectively ending the conversation. "We are hosting a ball tomorrow night, and we would love to have you in attendance." My jaw clenched so hard, I swore one of my teeth cracked. I had no interest in attending a ball. They were crowded and stuffy, with rigid dancing and fake smiles. It seemed they mostly served as either a place to flaunt wealth or play politics. Though I hated having to bend to the will of another, we could not go without that shipment much longer, and I knew I needed to tread carefully.

"We would be honored," I said, ensuring my tone was void of any displeasure.

"Excellent," Yvon said. "We can meet more in the coming days and be sure sufficient security has been reached."

We were led to our rooms by servants. I paid attention to my surroundings, taking note of where guards sat, invisible.

When we finally reached our destination, I thanked the people who led us and slipped into my room. It was average, with a large bed and a small desk.

There was a light knock at the door. Though I didn't want to, I got up and answered it. Damyr stood on the other side, smirking easily. "How did the meeting go?" he asked.

"Fine. Hopefully, things will get settled quickly."

He looked at me for a moment. "Do you truly think that, or is that just what you're telling yourself?"

I huffed in amusement. "If I don't tell myself that, what else would I have?"

"Fair enough. Want to go into town to grab a bite for lunch?"

"No, thank you," I said. "I'm going to rest after our travel. I'm sure there will be many meetings ahead."

"Sounds good. I'll see you later, then."

As he turned, I stopped him. "We were also invited to attend a ball tomorrow night."

I sat down and stared out the window. Exhaustion sat deep in my bones. Most days felt like I was being buried under a mountain of sand, sitting right in the middle of my chest, constantly pressing, weighing me down until I could no longer take it. Though this meeting seemed like a glimmer of hope, it all still felt like, eventually, it would come crashing down. I felt beyond desperate but had no idea how else to fix it.

From my window I could see the training yard. Knights and trainees were there, running around a track, sparring and weight-lifting. It seemed they had impressive equipment and a decent regiment. It was easy to tell who was fresh to training and who had been there for a while.

One match in particular caught my attention. I couldn't make out faces from here, but one of them had dark hair, the other dusky blond. The blond was large for a human, but it seemed he lacked much wit. The smaller one with dark hair took them out in a second.

Another one entered the ring. They were more evenly matched, but the one with darker hair took them out quickly. Over and over again, the human with dark hair threw people down to the mat, ones their size and smaller. I was impressed, not only at the ability, but the stamina.

Though I felt drawn to watch longer, I was exhausted and knew I needed to prepare for tomorrow. I flopped down on the bed and closed my eyes.

Chapter Two

SORCHA

My sword clanked against Jareyth's, the sound ringing around the training yard. He tried to gain leverage with his strength, the brute always tried to throw his weight around. I parried him away easily, and he backed off, circling, planning his attack.

I waited back, getting a read on his next move. I'd been sparring for a while, back-to-back. He was trying to take advantage of my tiredness, but I barely felt it. In the ring like this, it felt like the world was silent. The sounds of others fighting and training in the yard fell away, leaving only me and Jaryeth. His breathing was labored, already tired from going all out in the beginning. His eyes bounced around me, deciding what to do. "Come at me, Yulean," he called, trying to bait me.

I didn't take it. I barely even heard him, focused on where his eyes traveled. As soon as he made his decision, his brows moved slightly, giving away his plan. Right then, he faked left, going right.

I leaned my weight to the side, throwing him off balance before I lunged forward, pushing hard and sending him backwards. He fell on his ass, and I pointed my practice sword at his neck, a smirk across my face.

He scoffed and flicked my sword aside. "Whatever. You got lucky."

I sheathed my sword. "Yeah, you wish." I hadn't lost a sparring match in over a year.

He stood and brushed himself off, acting like he didn't get his ass kicked. I stepped out of the circle, only to be approached by my commander, Hendrix.

"You had great technique, Yulean," he said, "but you left yourself open on your left when you threw him off balance. If you were against someone with matching wit, they would have taken the chance."

I nodded, taking in his words. "I'll work on that." Though Jaryeth didn't take the opportunity, I wasn't foolish enough to think someone else might not.

He glanced around me to Jareyth, who was now walking towards us.

"Pierce," Captain acknowledged. "Can you tell me where you went wrong?"

Jareyth huffed like a petulant child. "I let her get me off balance."

"Yes, but it was because you were only relying on your strength. There is much more to combat than physical strength, which you should know by now."

Jareyth's head hung, and his jaw tightened. "Yes, Captain."

Hendrix turned around. "Line up, men," he called. I tried not to flinch at that. I knew I was the only woman and it was a simple thing, but it was still a slight I felt deep in my bones. "Training is over for today. Pierce and Cade, you have the morning watch at the main gate. Smith and

Kain, you have night watch in tower three. The rest of you are dismissed until training tomorrow. Get some rest."

"Yes, sir," we all responded in unison.

As I packed up my things, Jareyth approached me again, hovering over me. "Looking to get your ass kicked again?" I asked him.

He scoffed. "It's funny someone who doesn't have to take guard shifts thinks she has any room to talk."

I ball my fists, trying not to let his effect show. "I have other responsibilities," I defended, keeping my tone level.

"Whatever you say. Oops, better not disrespect you, right? Could get me fired. That's why no one treats you the same."

I balled my hands into fists. There was no point in arguing with him, mostly because he was right. No matter how many times I won in the sparring ring or proved myself in technicals, I would never be equal to them.

I was still just a princess.

"Sorcha," a voice called. As if to prove my point, my sister Sybil stood on the edge of the training yard. She wore a light blue dress, her brown hair back in a tightly braided bun. Her personal guard, Holland, stood a few feet behind her, as he always did. Her shadow. He was a dragon who'd been her guard since we were young. "We need to be going."

Jareyth gave me a victorious grin before sauntering back towards the locker rooms.

I stood and grabbed my bag, heading over to my sister. All eyes were on us, and I could feel them boring into my back. "Yes?" I asked through clenched teeth.

Her brow rose. "It's nearly dinner time," she said. "And we're supposed to have it together. I thought you may get...distracted and forget."

I pinched my nose with my fingers. I had forgotten. Our mothers instated family dinner at least twice a week. Though I enjoyed spending time with them, it took me away from this, which they did enough.

"I didn't," I lied.We began walking back into the castle, my training boots clicking against the marble floors. I looked at the balcony above on the second floor, knowing guards were posted beside the four pillars, as well as a few hidden among the walls. What I wouldn't give to be in their position. But instead, I was walking the halls pretending they weren't there, that they were nonexistent.

We made it to my room. I kept it simple, with cream walls and very little decoration. I never had plans to stay here, so there was no point in customizing.

"I'm going to find Sage and make sure she's ready for tonight. Can I trust you to be on time?" Sybil asked

"Yeah. Thanks, mom," I said. Sybil only nodded and left, her shadow behind her, his blue wings tucked tight and his curly horns sticking out above his silvery white hair.

After I bathed, I put on a pair of loose-fitting pants and a basic tunic. Normally, I would do what was expected and put on a dress, but I couldn't be bothered today. I knew I would get stares, but no more than normal. Ever since I showed interest in training with the knights, I've been looked at oddly.

I walked from my room to the main dining room, where I was sure everyone else was. As I traversed the halls, all the areas where knights sat on guard weighed on me. I knew they all saw me, knew I was a fraud. I felt like one.

When I got there, my mothers and Sybil were already there. I sat next to Sybil and noticed Mom eyeing my pants as I approached. It was fifty-fifty on whether she would mention them, based on her glance back to Sybil, she was going to keep it to herself.

I released a deep breath. "Where's your sister?" Mother asked after a moment.

Sybil looked towards the door. "I checked in, and she said she was coming. I can go get her."

She moved to get up, but Mama waved her off. "I'll send someone. You know how she can be."

As if on cue, Sage bound through the room, her blonde hair straight and her bangs hanging in her eyes. She had on a light pink gown, her favorite color.

"You're late," Sybil said. "You said you'd be here."

She looked confused. "You told me I had a few minutes."

"That was half an hour ago. You need to manage your time better."

Sage narrowed her eyes. "It's not my fault you were so unclear." She plopped down angrily in her chair, crossing her arms.

"A few minutes is a concise–"

"Girls," Mama cut in. "Why don't we stop fighting and eat?"

Food was quickly served, and everyone dug in, staying relatively silent.

"Oh, Sorcha," Mama said, turning her attention to me. "How was training today?"

"Fine," I said. "I nailed a new technique that allows for easier kills if you need to go in for hand-to-hand."

They silenced around me, but I continued eating. I only got asked occasionally, and this was why.

"That sounds nice," Mama said, trying to be encouraging.

Mother cleared her throat and turned to my sister. "So what do we know of the situation in Valcor?"

My ears perked up, but I kept my focus on my food. When I showed too much interest, they tended to stop talking.

"I'm not sure. If he's to be believed, either information got out about the route of the transfer, or it was a thieving troupe who stumbled over it by accident. But that's if he's to be believed."

Mother seemed to contemplate that for a moment. "Do we think they're being truthful?"

"Perhaps," Sybil continued. "Requesting a meeting would be strange if it was him, but we should be on our guard. He could be hoarding them for some other reason." Sybil had been training to become queen since birth. It was what she was destined to do, and it had nothing to do with her being next in line. She was sharp but kind, the perfect mix for a leader. Mother had been giving her more responsibilities as of late, and this was just another one of those.

"Hopefully, with more careful observation, we can learn more."

I had to bite my tongue. There were a million ways I could think to help, different tactical moves we could make, but I knew saying anything would just end in rejection.

"If it was a random group of bandits, it's strange none of the stones have appeared on the black market," Mother continued.

"Do you mean magestones?" I asked, unable to stop myself.

They all looked at me, and I made sure to keep my face neutral, to not give away too much.

"Yes," my mother said eventually. "We have the King of Valcor visiting after a shipment went missing."

"And he's behind it?" I asked.

"We're not jumping to conclusions," Mama said evenly. "We're trying to hear him out. He seemed to be truly unaware."

I drank in every word they said, memorizing the details. Even with my extensive training, we never learned much about Valcor. They were a nation comprised mostly of Minotaurs and largely kept to themselves. Our mothers went to visit once, briefly, when the newest king was picked, but I had never seen him, nor had I been to Valcor. All I knew was they were a country with a lot of tradition and a history in battle.

But they were right, targeting trade routes wouldn't be something a king with a plan for war would do. Then what was going on? I turned it over in my head, trying to figure it out. I wanted to suggest sending people to do recon while their king was away, but I knew where that would lead.

"Goddess above," Sage said, pushing food around her plate. "Can we talk about anything else? Who cares?"

"You should care," Mother said. "Though you're not in line to rule, it's still your kingdom."

Sage scoffed. "Well, I don't."

Mama changed the topic to appease Sage and avoid a fight between her and Mother, but my mind stayed focused on what could be going on. Dinner finished relatively quickly, and I planned to go to the yard to blow off some steam.

As I took my leave, Mother called my name from behind me.

I froze. Sybil and Sage had already left, Sybil to get some work done and Sage to go to another ball with her friends. "Yes, Mother?" I said.

"I would appreciate you dressing appropriately for the ball tomorrow night. We need to make a good impression."

My jaw tightened. I had forgotten about the ball, just another torturous thing to do. Another way to be shown off as different. "Sure. Can I go? I'm exhausted."

She eyed me before nodding, and I left, my thrumming footsteps echoing off the marble. I could feel the eyes of the guards on me as I walked, knights I trained with and worked with, all doing their jobs while I was here, expected to attend extravagant parties and get shipped off to marriage someday.

All I'd ever wanted was to become a knight. Since I was old enough to pick up a toy sword, I knew that was what I wanted to do. I used to sit in my lessons and stare out the window, watching the training yard, yearning to be there. When I turned sixteen, of age to start training in the ranks, I begged my mothers to let me join. I'd been asking for years, and by the time we were there, I had whittled them down enough to say yes.

I would go to my lessons, then every day when they were done, I would train, working hard to improve my skills. I was sure my parents were secretly working against me. Suddenly, my tutor insisted I needed to spend more time in class after lessons, planning more events and meetings I had to attend. Luckily, whenever I had time to practice, Hendrix would help me, telling me I showed promise, teaching me the technique I was lacking.

By the time practicals started in the spring, my mothers thought I would have given up. Until then, nothing had caught my interest the way sparring did, so they assumed I would give it up before I even got started.

I nailed my practical. I was third on the list to join the ranks and ecstatic. A lot of the guys acted like I got in because I was royalty, or that others went easy on me for fear of injury, but I won on my own merit. Jareyth got waitlisted for a year and was still upset, which was why he picked a fight with me any chance he could. Too bad I threw him to the mat every time.

Even though I was twenty-two now, plenty old enough to be a real knight, I wasn't granted any of the real jobs that came with it. I'd never been able to take a watch or patrol the town, much less seen battle. It was like I was playing pretend all the time, and I was sick of it.

My parents insisted it was too dangerous to send me out, that enemies would target me to get to them. When I suggested being able to keep watch in the castle, they denied me again. How would it look to the other royal families for a princess to stand watch? That was what it all seemed to boil down to, public perception.

So for now, I stuck to the training ring, waiting for my opportunity to prove to them I was more useful on the battlefield than I was in a dress. Then, public perception be damned, they would have to let me fight.

I escaped to the yard, the cool, crisp fall air chilling my skin. Magestone lanterns lit the area as I moved around. No one was here, and it was my favorite time to learn a new skill. I'd been working on knife throws. It wasn't something I'd ever been proficient in, but I was determined to learn.

I grabbed the throwing knives from the stand and stood across from the target. I lined the knife up and took a deep breath. On my exhale, I released, sending the blade flying towards the target. It smacked it with a resounding thud, echoing through the empty space. It landed in the third ring on the right side.

As I went to throw the next one, I heard a rustling. Glancing around, I didn't see anyone, but I knew I heard it.

I heard it again, finally spotting movement over the fence. Large horns stuck out over the top, and my interest was piqued. What was a minotaur doing out and about this time of night? It made me recall what my mothers talked about over dinner. Was he looking for something? Spying?

I knew I should alert the guard, but the curiosity, mixed with this chance to potentially stop him myself, was too great to stop. I crept to the fence and snuck out the side gate, following after the minotaur.

Chapter Three

ZARIOS

After getting some rest, I did a quick loop of the palace, doing my best to look like any other visitor while memorizing more of the castle around me.

When I was done, I decided to walk the woods on the perimeter of the area. I could have stuck to the grounds, but I didn't want to be around more people than necessary. I grimaced thinking about the ball I already committed to attending.

As I stepped through the forest path, I heard a branch crack that wasn't from my steps. I continued walking, not letting on that I heard, but I was surely being followed. It wasn't surprising. If I was on the opposite side, I wouldn't be trusting either. Though I was no longer a general, I grew up to become one, and I knew how they thought.

A few minutes later, I caught them out of the corner of my eye. The glint of armor peered through the trees, moonlight bouncing off the metal. I huffed in amusement. They saw me as such a small threat, they couldn't even send someone trained? This person was obviously still new if they had that much trouble hiding in a dense forest.

I couldn't help it. I drew my sword, hoping to egg them on. I didn't hear any more movement, but the glint was gone.

I held my stance, circling around. Suddenly, I heard a slight noise that drew my attention. "I know you're there," I said, loud enough for them to hear.

I didn't hear anything else, so I kept walking. "Fine," I sighed, sheathing my sword. "If you want to enjoy a nice walk through the woods, be my guest. But watch out—I've heard there's some nasty thistle in there."When I said that, the bush to the right shook slightly. As it did, I took my opportunity. I swung my sword out and cut through the top. I knew I wouldn't hit whoever was there, I just wanted to mess with them a little, not cause any actual harm.

What I didn't expect was to be met with a readied blade, pushing mine away and out of my grip. I didn't have the sturdiest hand when I swung, not expecting any kind of retaliation.

Out of the bush came a head of dark hair and pale skin that looked familiar, but I couldn't recall why. She was beautiful, her face sharp, and she wore knight's armor, but it seemed to be an unofficial set. Her eyes were piercing and dark, like there was a fire behind them.

"Don't move," she said, her sword now pointed at my neck. Her voice was deep and melodic.

I huffed my annoyance. "I was just trying to take a walk."

"Then why did you swing at me?"

I smirked. "Because you aren't very good at your job."

"I am," she said in disbelief.

"I easily saw you, so I would have to disagree."

Her grip let up slightly. "How—"

I took my opportunity, pushing her sword away as I reached for the dagger still at my side. She recovered quickly, jumping from the bush and readying up in front of me.

Her frame was small, barely reaching my chest. Her sword was also much smaller than mine, with a purple gem in the hilt. Though it was fancy, it was obviously also practical. She was in training armor, her hair pushed back off her face.

"What are you doing here?" I asked.

"I could ask the same question," she said.

I moved forward, like I would slash at her, but she blocked it easily.

I swung again, harder this time, and again, her blade bounced mine away. I had no intention of harming her, but for some reason, I couldn't help but play with her a bit. It was obvious she was trained, despite lacking any snooping abilities.

"You're better than you look," I commented.

She blew a piece of hair from her face. "I've heard that a few times."

She went in for the attack this time, going for my non-dominant side. I blocked her, swinging her off and sending her flying. She landed with an oof, her ass hitting the leafy ground.

She got up with grace and ran at me again, this time aiming lower in hopes I couldn't block. Though I was large, I was much more dexterous than my opponents ever gave me credit for. I blocked her before going for a counter she blocked flawlessly.

We went back and forth, trading blow for blow, neither of us ever quite getting the advantage. It had been a very long time since I met someone who could match me in this way. Even when I trained with the guard, I was always going at about half. Here, I was going full out, needing to use my strength *and* my mind to its fullest. Though the fierce look never left her face, I could tell she was also enjoying this fight.

Finally, I managed to get a bit of an upper hand, catching her off guard and sweeping her to the ground. Her sword dropped a bit away, and I was on her before she could scramble for it. I dropped my dagger and gripped her hands above her head, breathing heavily. Her breasts shook slightly with the action, my cock taking definite notice. I ignored it. I hadn't gotten laid in a while, and I was sure that was the reason.

"Were you sent on orders to follow me?" I asked. I needed to know how much scrutiny I was truly under.

Her eyes narrowed, her lips shut tight. Even pinned under me, she never relented. "Suit yourself." I pulled my belt from its place around my waist.

Her eyes widened. "What are you doing?"

"Nothing of that sort," I promised.

She started trying to break free once again, but it was no use. I tied her hands above her head. Seeing her laid out, tied up with a red face, was doing things to me, things I would never admit aloud.

"Free me this instant," she insisted, still struggling. I stood up and pulled her to her feet before picking up both of our swords, all the while leading her with the tail of my belt.

I began the trek back to the castle, but she fought me harshly still. "You don't need to be difficult," I told her, but she kept fighting. "Fine," I said after a few moments of fighting, "but you chose this."

I walked towards her, and her eyes widened. "What are you doing?" she said, trying and failing again to escape. I caught her as I yanked the belt forward, before throwing her over my shoulder easily, her legs dangling in front of me.

She screamed and began kicking me, slapping my back with her fists. "Fighting will just tire you out," I told her.

She continued for a few moments more before relaxing, realizing my words were true. "You can't take me back like this. They'll think you've kidnapped me." I found it interesting that she sounded more nervous than angry.

"If they see me," I said.

"There are guards everywhere. Someone will see you. Just put me down. I'll walk with you."

There was a hint of worry in her tone again. "Someone sounds embarrassed to get caught."

I felt her punch into my back again. "It's not about that. Put me down!"

"Don't worry, I won't let you get caught." It was obvious to me she didn't want to be caught by her captain. She must have come to the force recently.

She scoffed. "Are you going to carry me the whole way?"

"Yes." And it wasn't because she felt right in my arms.

"Great."

Chapter Four

SORCHA

THIS WAS HUMILIATING. I was hanging off his shoulder, my ass in the air and my hands tied with a belt. He'd walked us out of the woods to the edge of the courtyard. Though I wanted to scream and fight, I knew that wasn't in my best interest. He was right. Not only would I get in trouble for getting caught, but this was embarrassing. I was so sure I had him back there, but he surprised me. I was used to brutes like him only using their strength and underestimating me, but once the fight got going, he became a very worthy opponent.

I shouldn't have followed him in the first place. I was sure Mother would have a few choice words about this. It was probably enough to have me thrown from training. My gut sank at the thought. It felt like I was handed an opportunity to show what I was capable of, and I fucked it up.

As he got to the castle, he somehow managed to stick to invisible walls and passages, avoiding even the places guards hid. How did an outsider who just arrived today know all of this? It only made my suspicion grow.

He even knew where the servants' corridor was that led right to his room.

When we got there, he put me down on the desk chair, latching the belt to it so my hands were stuck behind my back. All the guest rooms in the castle were the same, with some kind of painting of Peradona landscapes, a four-poster bed with heavy curtains, a desk, and a small couch on the side. This one had a painting of the juneberry orchard in Shimer. Juneberries only grew for a few weeks in the summer and made my favorite candy. Mama always made sure to get me some while they were in season.

"How did you do that?" I asked, unable to help it.

He unsheathed both of our swords, putting them on the bed, far out of my reach. "Do what?"

"Sneak past all the guards. Even the hidden ones."

He shrugged casually. "Can't go giving away all my secrets, can I?"

I sat there, staring at him.

"Who are you?" he asked.

I didn't know how to answer. Did I tell the truth? Should I lie? He would find out tomorrow anyway, but he couldn't tell my mothers.

"Don't want to answer that either?" he asked when I said nothing. "Fine. I'm sure if I ask the guard at the end of the hall, he'll tell me." He started walking towards the door. "Stop," I said.

He paused and looked at me, waiting. I sighed. "Fine. I'm Sorcha."

"Sorcha?" he said, the syllables rolling over his tongue. He approached me and bent so we were level. I let myself take a long look at him. He was all black with white bangs hanging over his eyes, blocking his expression from me.

Though his eyes were barely visible, I could tell they were dark. His snout was long, and he had a strong jaw. His horns curved up above his head, making his big frame appear somehow even more massive. It was hard to tell outside in the dark, but he was much larger than I thought. Even for a minotaur, he was giant. Though he wasn't human by any means, he was very attractive.

"Do you mean Princess Sorcha Yulean?" he asked.

I flinched.

"I thought you seemed familiar. This just got even more interesting."

My eyes narrowed. "Can you please just let me go? I'm sorry I followed you. Please, just don't tell your king." If he told him, he would definitely tell my parents.

He huffed from his nose. "I don't serve anyone," he said. "I am Grand Clarak of Valcor." My eyes widened. "Wait. You're King Zarios Kalimore?"

"I am no king," he snapped. He obviously had issues with titles. "But yes, I am Grand Clarak Zarios Kalimore of Ashmore."

Shit. I wasn't just following anyone—I was following their king, or Grand Clarak, whatever. I was done for. Though I didn't know what the exact situation was, I knew things were rocky, and I didn't want to cause any more tension.

"I apologize for following you," I said through gritted teeth. "I was in the training yard and got curious. I didn't know who you were." This was humiliating, but I had to make this right. Maybe if I didn't trigger an all-out war, I wouldn't be banned from training.

He leaned on the bed across from me, his arms back, holding him up, his hooves crossed in front of him. I could see the muscles of his arms bulge as he did. Moons, he was large.

I mentally shook myself. I couldn't be ogling my captor, no matter how massive he was.

After a moment that went on for far too long, he nodded. "I accept your apology, princess. I would be interested as well. Why were you in the training yard?"

"I don't see how that's any of your business," I said flatly.

He huffed again, but this one sounded different than before. "You have a lot of attitude for someone who was caught. Easily, might I add."

Anger welled up inside me. "It wasn't easy," I asserted. "I could kick your ass if we went again."

The corner of his lip turned up. "I would take your bet on that."

We stared at each other, tension sparking between us. "Why are you here?" I asked. I shouldn't have. I knew I shouldn't have, but I couldn't help it—the question just tumbled out.

"You haven't been told?" he asked.

"I have." At least, mostly. "But I want to hear it from you."

He sighed, relaxing further into the bed. "If I tell you, will you answer an inquiry I have?"

I thought about it. "I will try," I said honestly.

"Very well. The magestones you ship to us are very important. Without them, we can't run our forges anymore, and we need the shipment you're holding."

My head cocked. "We don't have it."

He froze. "What?"

I wanted to put all the words back into my mouth. "What did you say?" he repeated, more insistent this time.

"We sent the shipment already. It went missing." I had no idea they didn't tell him. I assumed that was what they were in negotiations about.

He seemed to turn that over for a little while. I wiggled in the restraints a bit, but more to give me something to do than out of discomfort.

"I was under the impression it was never sent because of the attacks."

"Attacks?" I asked.

He nodded. "We've had quite a few assaults on foreign shipments over the last few months. I assumed it was just a particularly large group of thieves, but..." He trailed off.

"But what?" "Magestones are shipped on a separate route, one that's only used for that once inside Valcor. Only the Claraks know about it, save for me of course."

"Claraks?" I asked.

He sighed, as if annoyed I wasn't all caught up on the inner workings of Valcor politics. "I am the Grand Clarak," he explained. "I rule over Valcor and its Capital, Ashmore. There are three other major territories, Sobury, Thvetharion, and Mertis." He ticked them off on his fingers. "They are all run by their own Clarak, who oversees that land."

I nodded. "So, you and the Claraks were the only ones who could have known about the shipment?"

"Yes, which means these aren't just random thieves. They're targeted, and they're coming from one of the rulers of my land. This is a full-out rebellion I'm dealing with, not just a stubborn band of criminals."

For the first time being around him, I felt like I could read him. Defeat took over his entire stance.

"Can't you investigate them?" I asked, trying to help. "You said earlier you assumed one of your Claraks was involved. Why not search there?"

"How?" he asked. "Though I am Grand Clarak, I can't just go in there, demanding to look through their things."

"Why? That's the whole point of being king."

He pinched the bridge of his snout in irritation. "Because I'm not a king, despite what you Peradonians think. I am a Grand Clarak, and we have to follow a different set of rules."

I turned that over in my mind. "Can't you just visit them? Come up with a reason and drop in, then spy?"

"That would be too suspicious," he said. "Claraks always come to the castle, not the other way around. The only time that happens is when..."

His words died on his tongue. I could see the gears turning and stayed quiet, letting him think.

"Princess," he finally said to my disgruntlement. "Why were you following me? That is my question."

It felt as if his gaze bore through me, looking into my soul. I felt he was right, a truth for a truth. "I want to be a knight. I *am* a knight. I just need to prove it to my mothers. I thought if I caught you doing something you shouldn't, it might be my chance to make them see I was capable."

That was the first time I'd ever said any of it aloud. It made me feel raw but also free. Someone else knew. He continued his thinking, soon pacing.

"What if I told you we could help each other?"

I was skeptical. "Continue."

"There is one way I could visit all the Claraks, but I can't do it alone. I need company. That's where you come in."

I didn't understand his meaning. "You need a guest?"

He sighed. "This is going to sound outlandish, but just...listen before you deny me."

I nodded, unsure where he was going with that.

"Whenever a Grand Clarak gets an intended mate, there's a ceremony that takes place that includes being hosted by every Clarak. They give their blessing, and the royal couple move to the next location. If we were to pretend you were my intended mate, we'd be able to sneak around and find the evidence we need."

My mouth hung open, my eyes wide. He wanted... "You want me to be your fiancée?" I asked in disbelief.

"Fake fiancée," he clarified, as if it made a difference. "Then you could come back and prove you solved the case, showing you can be a knight. It's a win-win."

I shut my mouth. What he was saying made sense, but it seemed absurd. "No one would believe us," I argued.

"Of course they would," he said. "I'm planning to be here for a week. In that time, we can craft a whirlwind love story good enough to convince your parents you want to marry me."

He was right about that, but could I really? If we pulled this off, if I helped save Valcor from a potential rebellion, there was no way they could turn me down to become a knight. At that point, I would probably be able to lead my own unit.

I whined. "Fine, fine. I agree. But only if we're believable enough before we leave."

His lip lifted into a small smirk. "Excellent. Let's talk about what needs to be done."

I swallowed. I wasn't sure if this would even be possible. My mothers were very attentive, not to mention my sisters. We would need to be extremely convincing.

"Fine, but untie me," I insisted. "It's not a good look to have your intended mate tied up."

He approached, his large frame towering over me. "I think it's an excellent look." He loosened the belt until it came free.

My face heated, but I ignored it and stood.

We had much to plan before tomorrow.

CHAPTER FIVE

SORCHA

I SLIPPED ON MY deep maroon ball gown and allowed one of the maids to do my hair. It was all tucked into a braid that formed a crown around my head. I even wore a slight bit of rouge I borrowed from Sage. She looked at me like I had three heads but didn't ask further questions. Everything had to go right.

We planned to make this our first real meeting, and we needed to play it up, make sure everyone saw us.

With one last deep breath, I made my way to the ballroom. I could hear the music and chatter of voices as I approached. My palms were sweaty. Though I had snuck around and skirted the rules, I'd never outright lied to my parents, and especially not my sisters. But I couldn't tell them. I couldn't take that risk.

The room was packed, royals and nobles milling around. A band played in the corner, and magestone lanterns were set to a low dim, bathing the room in a soft light. "Sorcha," my mama said once she spotted me. "You look lovely." She looked elegant in her sapphire gown, gems dripping from the skirt, making her sparkle as she turned. Her laugh lines were deep as she smiled at me, created by all the other times she had.

I hugged her. "You do too. Where's Mother?" I asked.

"Over there," she pointed. I could see my mother's dark hair sticking out of the crowd. "She's speaking with the Duke of Atrune." She leaned in further, speaking low. "That man is a terrible bore. I had to get out of there, and your mother was just an unfortunate casualty of my escape."

I giggle. "Mama, that's horrible!"

She laughed and shrugged. "That's what love is for. One day, you'll see."

"There you are," my mother said as she found us. "How dare you do that to me? I had to have a twenty-minute conversation about horse racing."

Mama giggled. "And you survived somehow." Mother tried to look angry, but she couldn't help but smile. "You owe me."

"Whatever you say," Mama said with a smirk.

I smiled. Though we didn't see eye-to-eye about a lot of things, I loved my parents. They had always been so kind and loving, and seeing their love taught me what a good, healthy relationship looked like.

Which made the idea of lying to them even harder, but it had to be done. One day, they would understand.

It didn't take me long to spot Zarios in the crowd. He towered over everyone. Though there were many other beings here—fae, lizardmen, a few dragons—there was no one who matched him in height.

Last time I saw him, he was shirtless, but tonight, he wore a white dress shirt that looked as if it would rip if he breathed too heavily and the same kind of tight trousers he wore before. His hair still hung over his eyes, but it was all neatly brushed. Even his fur looked shiner. Though I hated to admit it, he cleaned up nicely.

He made eye contact with me, and I froze. I didn't even know how I knew he was looking at me, I couldn't see his eyes. It was almost as if I could *feel* rather than see his gaze.

I broke the connection and moved to the bar, hoping he'd take the hint. Though we planned a public meeting here, there wasn't any discussion on how everything would play out.

I stood, pretending to peruse the drink menu.

"Can I get you a drink?" that deep voice I recognized said.

I turned and had to tilt my chin up to look at him. "It's an open bar," I said with an arched eyebrow.

He shrugged. "It's not really about the drink, is it? Just a way to start a conversation."

"And you wanted to speak with me?"

"Very much."

My face heated, and that had nothing to do with our rouse. "I'll take that drink," I said evenly.

He gestured for the bartender and ordered us each an ale. Though I would normally sip wine at these events, I'd spent plenty of nights downing ale with the other recruits and actually preferred it. We were each handed a tankard, and I took a sip, the bubbly bitter taste rolling over my tongue.

"I don't think I caught your name," I said.

He smirked, playing into our little game. "I am Grand Clarak Zarios of Valcor."

"Grand Clarak?" I said as if I was confused. "That's an interesting title. Is it like a king?"

He huffed, and his tail whipped behind him, as if he were irritated. "Not exactly, but I am considered ruler of the land."

I had to fight to contain my laugh at his reaction. "Nice to meet you. I'm Princess Sorcha Yulean."

"Nice to meet you, Princess," he said.

"No need to be so formal. Sorcha is fine."

"Whatever you say, Princess."

It was my turn to look irritated. He smirked behind his glass before taking a sip. I downed half the tankard, needing a small hit of courage. This would be simple. Get to know him. Make sure others see.

Easy.

"Would you like to dance?" I asked.

He looked to the dance floor. "Not really."

Irritation fell on my features. "Are you sure I can't convince you? It would be nice to dance with everyone else." I tried to make the last part pointed, to convey my meaning. We *needed* people to see us dancing together.

It seemed he finally got the message. With a sigh, he threw back his tankard, chugging it all in one go. "Lead the way."

Instinctually, I grabbed his hand. It was large and wrapped around mine. When we reached the dance floor, he pulled me in, bringing me towards his body. I landed against him, throwing my other hand up to steady myself. It fell against his broad chest. Though he had a shirt on, I could feel the texture of his fur beneath it. It wasn't what I was used to, it did feel nice.

He swayed us around, easily taking the lead. "I see you've had some dance experience," I commented.

"A bit," he said. "My mother thought it was important for a proper man to know how to dance."

"So did my tutor," I said. "She told us once that if a man leads you in a dance and he misses the steps, move on."

His brow raised behind his bangs. "That seems a bit intense."

"It is," I confirmed. "She was intense. She also said if a man is truly interested in you, it's normal for him to act mean to you."

"That seems like it sends a bad message."

"I agree."

"I guess I better not mess up this dance then," he said with a smirk. "I wouldn't want to send you away when things were just getting interesting."

We swayed around the space, falling into step with each other easily. His hand was wrapped firmly around my waist, keeping me close to his warm body. I tended not to dance at these events, preferring to stand in the back and mingle when I must, but I found I was enjoying myself.

"Ready?" he asked.

"Ready for what?"

He didn't answer. I braced when he suddenly swung me around, spinning me out towards the crowd and back into his body before dipping us down.

When I came back up, I felt breathless. "What do you think your tutor would have thought of that?" he asked.

"That you were much too showy for your own good," I said.

He laughed, the sound rattling through his body and vibrating against mine. "That may be fair."

We danced to a few more songs, and I saw people start to take notice. Sage had outright stared as if we were a spectacle, and I knew my mothers saw me. When I looked, neither of them seemed to react, but they did glance our way a few times, whispering back and forth.

"I think our plan is working," I said, whispering into his ear.

"I thought it might." I scoffed. "Are you always this humble?"

"Another reason I'm such a catch," he said with a wink.

I snorted a laugh. What was wrong with this man?

After one more, I needed a break. He led me back to the bar, where we ordered more drinks. We sat around, talking about nothing. I was sure to lightly touch him occasionally, pushing his shoulder playfully and resting my hand on his. Though I had never tried to seduce a man, I'd watched Sage do it successfully for years and managed to pick up a thing or to.

Soon, the party began to wind down, and the room started to clear. "Can I walk you to your rooms?" he asked once our last round of drinks were done.

My brow quirked. "Seems a bit presumptuous, don't you think?"

"I only have interest in your conversation," he replied easily.

"Then I suppose I could allow it." He put out his arm, and I took it easily. I caught Sybil staring at us through the corner of my eye as we left. Great. Everyone had seen, and part one seemed to go according to plan.

The halls were dimly lit and empty, the two moons shining their light through the windows, casting the sky in a pink and blue glow.

"Do you think they believed us?" I asked once I was sure we were alone.

"Of course. My acting is great. And you were so flustered, even I began to believe you."

I smacked his arm, the sound echoing through the corridor. "I was not flustered."

"Whatever you need to tell yourself, Princess."

"Please quit calling me that," I grumbled.

"I think it has a nice ring to it," he replied.

I let out an irritated sigh, but soon, we were at my door. "I have training tomorrow, but I was thinking we could meet for lunch and walk in the garden after morning session."

"That would be good. I saw many people in the courtyard today, so it seems that would be a good place to be seen."

When I opened my door, he followed slightly until he was leaning against the door frame. He took a slight peak into my room, but he wouldn't find anything of note.

"See you tomorrow, Princess," he said. And then, he was gone.

When the door clicked shut, I leaned against the back, letting my head rest on the cool wood. Moons, this whole thing was ridiculous. I fought around until I managed to get my dress off, not wanting to call a maid to help me. I'm pretty certain I tore something, but I didn't care.

It felt like I was walking right into the life I didn't want. Being courted by royalty and attending balls. And Zarios didn't make it any easier. He was so sure of himself, so sure this plan would fall right into place. Not to mention exasperating.

Though I was playing the role I despised now, I needed to remember it was all to get what I wanted. After this was over, I would become a knight and never have to attend another silly ball or be expected to marry to enhance the bonds of a kingdom. It would all be worth it, it had to be.

After removing every pin in my hair and taking a shower I threw myself down on my bed, ready for this all to be over. As I laid there, I realized we'd walked all that way hand in hand with no one watching.

CHAPTER SIX

ZARIOS

I SPENT THE MORNING gazing out at the training yard. I watched Sorcha go through her motions. She did some conditioning then moved to working out. They then broke off into skills, and I smirked as she threw at least four men down to the mat. Her movements were swift and precise. It was impressive. Something about seeing her like this, as opposed to the princess in a gown I'd seen last night, attracted me even more. Though none of this was meant to be real, the attraction to her wouldn't need to be faked.

It also made me realize she was the only woman there. That must have been a tough position to be in, but she seemed to hold her own.

A while later, Kiaza came to take us to another meeting. It ended with more of the same. I told my side of the story over again, and they never admitted to already sending the magestones. Without Sorcha, I would have had no clue, but now that I did, I was irritated. I was being kept here and observed, waiting to see if they trusted me enough to send another shipment.

I couldn't say anything, though. If I did, it would give away our plans, which I couldn't have. Though getting the stones were important, ending the mutiny I felt rising took priority.

After the uneventful meeting, I left to make my way to the garden.

"Wait," I heard as I moved down the hall.

When I turned, I found Sybil Yulean. Her dragon guard stood behind her but stopped a few feet away, offering her some privacy. Though dragons did have excellent hearing, so maybe it was to give her the illusion of privacy.

"How can I help you?" I asked.

She gave me a scrutinizing look, but I didn't waver. Years of being raised like a soldier taught me not to crack under such a thing.

"I'll get to the point," she said. "What are you doing with my sister?"

"I'm sorry?" I asked.

"Everyone saw you dancing last night. She has never shown interest in...well, anyone. What are your intentions?"

Never? The thought stirred something in me that shouldn't be there, something possessive.

I shrugged, hiding my true feelings. "No intentions. I just found her interesting and decided to keep her company."

She continued to examine me. "If there's nothing else," I said, "I have a prior engagement to make."

As I continued to walk, she called out, "Don't play with her. Though I'm not skilled with a sword as she is, he is," she pointed back towards the dragon, "and I will ensure it doesn't end well for you, if Sorcha doesn't first."

I paused before smirking. Though I normally didn't respect people who got their throne through bloodline, I liked her spark and her protectiveness over Sorcha. "Noted."

If only she knew what we truly had planned.

I found my way to the gardens. As I entered, I noticed a single red Yaisy, its five petals spread wide. Though the fall was creeping in, there were still a few flowers around. I picked it, thinking of Sorcha. That was a thing people did while courting a mate, so it seemed like a good idea.

Sorcha was already there, still in her training gear. Because it was all hand-to-hand, she was in a loose pair of trousers and a tunic. The trousers showed off her legs in a way I could appreciate.

When she saw me, she smiled, and it gave me pause. I had to keep in mind this was all a ruse. She was smiling at me, not *for* me. That smile was for all the others milling around, taking notice of my approach.

"Hello, Princess," I said when I was close enough.

Her eyes narrowed. "I wish you would stop calling me that."

I handed her the Yaisy. "It's what you are."

"For now," she muttered. I wanted to pry but decided this wasn't the place.

"I skipped breakfast but snagged this from the kitchen," she said, going to her bag.

She pulled out two bowls with lids.

I thanked her and popped mine open to eat. I'd missed breakfast observing the training and was starved. "This is very good," I said. It was a bowl of oats, mixed fruits, and a splash of honey.

"Right? It's my favorite. I have it for breakfast almost every day.""I can see why. How was training?"

She cocked her brow. "You're really curious?"

"Why wouldn't I be?"

She glanced away. "It was fine. We're working on hand-to-hand combos. I need to focus a bit more on my double leg takedown. It's not perfect yet."

"Those can be tricky to nail," I said. "It's all about where you're throwing your weight. People think it's all about strength, but it's not. It's more about balance. If you're sturdy, their opposite weight should be enough to throw them down."

I could see her imagining what I said, picturing the change in form. "That makes sense. I'll try that. How does a king know so much about fighting?"

"Not a king," I asserted. "But my father was the High General under the previous Grand Clarak. He taught me a lot from a very young age."

"That must be nice," Sorcha said.

"How so?" I wouldn't say I had a bad childhood, but I wasn't treated as a child for most of it. I was expected to act the way a general's son did, and I suppose that was like a soldier.

"I always wished I had been born into a more normal setting. It still may have been hard for me to become a knight, but I wouldn't have the literal rulers of the kingdom working against me."

She looked defeated. It was the first time I'd seen her look anything but confident. "It wasn't all rainbows," I said. "I never really had time to be young. Though I loved my parents, it was intense. Still, it molded me into the person I am today."

She took a bite, mulling over what I said. Soon, we were done with our lunch, just staring out at the gardens. They were pretty, with lots of flowers around and vines traveling around short fences. It reminded me of Sobury, but more organized and contained.

"Would you like to walk?" I asked her.

"That would be nice." I stood and put my hand out to help her up. She gazed at me, looking back to my hand before standing on her own, swiping at the non-existent wrinkles on her skirt. I let my hand drop and took my place by her side. Though it was strange she didn't take my hand, I decided to let it go. We were just acting, after all, and there was no need to worry over every little gesture.

After a few paces, we entered an enclosed pathway, lined with thick bushes on each side.

"Do you think it's working?" she asked quietly.

I couldn't hear any movement around, so I knew we were alone. "I believe so. I had a nice chat with your sister this morning."

She paused. "Sage?"

"No, Sybil."

Her face scrunched up in confusion. "Why?"

"She wanted to know my intentions." I could feel my tail whip a bit harder behind me of its own volition.

"What did you say?"

"I was interested, but we were just getting to know each other. She threatened me with her dragon guard if I hurt you."

She snorted, her face a bit red. "Yes, Sybil isn't afraid to wield Holland to her advantage. And he's even more willing to oblige."

"What's the deal with those two?" I asked. I'd never been particularly nosey, but his presence piqued my interest.

"I don't really know," she admitted. "When we were young, something happened, and then one day, he was here, shadowing her everywhere she went. At first, he was just training with the guard, but even then, when he wasn't at training, he was always right behind her until the day he finally finished academy and became her personal guard. Now, I rarely see them parted."

"Interesting." It was quite an odd situation, but sometimes, fate had a weird way of entangling people together.

"Maybe I could help you later," I said, my mind flitting elsewhere.

"With what?"

"Your takedown," I said. "I'm pretty good at them."

"Really?" she asked, seeming surprised.

"Yeah," I leaned in a bit. "It could help with our cause."

When I pulled away, she was slightly flushed. "That sounds like a plan."

Later that night, we met in the training yard. The set up was nice, with a running ring around the outside, sparring circles in the middle, and targets to the far end. Sorcha was on the other side, tying her hair back.

We stood in one of the sparring circles, the lights beating down on the space. The chilled night air breeze ruffled against my fur.

Sorcha began to lean this way and that, bending her limbs.

"What are you doing?" I asked.

She gave me a quizzical look. "Stretching?"

I huffed. "You can't stretch before battle."

She brought one arm across her chest, pulling her breasts together, accentuating them in a way I quickly took notice of. "But we aren't in battle," she said. "This is training, and it's better to prepare beforehand than be injured during training and weakest during a fight."

I considered her words. As I did, she bent down to stretch her legs. She lunged to one side, then the other, her back to me, her thigh stretched and her pants clinging to her body. It was as if my eyes were glued to her, unable to look away.

When she stood, I managed to pull my gaze elsewhere. My tail flicked behind me and my ears twitched slightly.

"Now I'm ready," she said.

"Perfect." I gestured her forward. "Show me what you got."

Determination set into her features, her eyes burning with confidence, she ran at me and wrapped her arms around me, trying to throw me off balance. I could feel her trying to force me with her legs instead of her core.

With ease, I twisted from her grip and grappled her, taking her down. We landed with a thud, but I was careful not to throw her with all my strength, cushioning her a bit with my arms.

"Again," she said, pushing against my chest.

I stood and moved across from her once more. "You need to use your core. You're only pushing with your legs, and it's easy to throw you off center like that."

"Got it." she seemed to really take in my words. I could see her slightly adjusting her weight while standing there to practice.

She came at me again and though I could feel the shift in her weight. Her core was much tighter, but she still wasn't able to throw me off balance. I once again spun us and threw her down.

I could see irritation building in her eyes. "Again."

So, we went again. And again, and again. Before I became Grand Clarak I helped train soldiers, and none of them worked harder than she did. She pushed herself harder every time. Though her tactics were improving, I was able to evade her on each attempt.

I'd thrown her down for the sixth time when she groaned in frustration. "You're just too big," I said. "I'll never be able to take you down."

I stood and tried to help her up again, but again, she batted my hand out of the way. "That's not true," I said.

"Of course it is," she said. "You're double my size, your strength makes it impossible."

"A great fighter doesn't blame their opponent for their shortcomings."

Her glare turned icy. "What's that supposed to mean?"

"My strength is not the reason you can't beat me. If you're not as strong, you always find another way to get ahead of your opponent. If they get the better of you, it is your fault, not theirs."

"I'm not saying you could beat me," she snapped. "I'm saying I can't throw you to the ground because you're heavy."

I smirked. "I believe the night we met, I was not the one being carried away."

"That's because you took me by surprise." she said. "Why don't we see now, on equal terms?"

My heart thudded in my chest, excited at the thought of going toe-to-toe with her once again. "Fine."

We both held our stance, neither ready to make a move. I decided to go first, swinging in for a grapple. She dodged me, moving to the side easily. As she did, she tried to sideswipe me with her shoulder, but I held firm, my balance still centered.

I threw a backhand she caught easily. Her leg swung up for a kick I easily dodged. We went back and forth, trading blows and dodging. Even though I was larger than her, she kept up with me, mostly on defense, but holding her own.

Until she went for a risky hook kick she didn't think I was prepared for. But I was—I caught her foot and twisted her, sending her flying to the mat. I then scrambled on top of her, pinning her down.

Our hard breathing and the singing of crickets were the only sounds around. I flopped down on the mat next to her, staring up at the stars and the moons. The large blue one had just appeared while the smaller pink one has almost made it halfway across the sky. They had names, but right now, I couldn't recall them.

"How was that, Princess?" I asked.

She smacked my shoulder. "You got lucky."

I huffed in amusement. "Whatever you have to tell yourself."

We laid there in silence, taking in the crisp fall night. "Ready to go inside?" Sorcha asked. "We wouldn't want to stay out too long and give the wrong impression."

"I suppose." I had forgotten about our little plan for a moment, just enjoying the training.

I got up and offered to help her, but she again ignored me. It was starting to get to me, but I, again, didn't say anything.

We each wiped off with a towel before heading inside. Though it was quiet, there were still a few people wandering around. Sorcha took my arm once we reached the first door, smiling easily the whole way.

As we neared her door, I heard light footsteps behind us. They followed us through most of the corridors.

I pulled Sorcha to my side, trying to appear a bit flirty. "Someone is following us."

She didn't look around to give us away but did pause. She leaned into me this time, but closer to my face, as if she would kiss me. My heart fluttered unexpectedly. "Once they get close enough, we'll ambush them."

"Got it," I breathed.

The steps rounded the corner, and we prepared to surprise them.

I could feel the mental countdown between us. *Three, two, one...*

We turned, her jumping behind them and me in front.

"Moons!" a woman's voice shouted.

I dropped my guard when I realized it was Sage, the youngest Yulean girl. "You didn't have to ambush me like that!" she squealed.

"What are you doing here?" Sorcha asked, not looking apologetic at all.

Sage pouted. "I was coming back from my party and saw you together. I just wanted to see what was going on since you've been so secretive."

Sorcha sighed. "Nothing is going on. We're just...spending time together."

She looked between us, a small smile touching her lips. "Right. Well, I'm going to go. I have someone to spend time with myself," she said with a wink. "Goodnight."

"Wait, who–" Before Sorcha could even get the words out, Sage was gone.

She sighed heavily. "That girl is more trouble than I am."

I let out a small chuckle. "I'm not sure that's possible."

She pushed me against my shoulder. "I can walk the rest of the way." She gestured to her door at the end of the hall. "Goodnight, King Zarios."

I grumbled. "Goodnight, Princess."

Chapter Seven

SORCHA

I PACED A HOLE in the floor, waiting for the meeting to start. It had been a week of Zarios and I sneaking off together, flirting, and making sure we were seen doing it. Word had begun to spread amongst the Lords and Ladies milling around the castle. The rumor mill was abuzz, exactly the way we wanted it.

My mothers had yet to say anything, but I'd been avoiding them, not wanting to break under their scrutiny. Sage and Sybil were less easy to doge, making their interest known in other ways. Sage asked me every time we crossed paths, and each time, I was sure to seem a bit more bashful than I was before. Sybil was much less straightforward, asking how my day was and inquiring about my plans, which she never had before.

But tonight was the night. There was a final meeting scheduled before Zarios left, and that was when we would tell them. I wasn't sure how things were going to go, how my mothers would take it, but I had to be confident and sell this. Not only would it help save Valcor, but saving a whole kingdom would show them I could handle being a knight. A real one.

After Zarios and I discussed how the meeting would go, I went to my room to pack. He told me I didn't need much. I'd thrown in a few dresses and undergarments, my toiletries, my armor, my sword, and at the last moment, a few pairs of pants and tops. Though I knew next to nothing about Valcor, I knew generally what was expected of women. I still grabbed them, however, just in case.

When I was done, I shoved my few bags under the bed. I didn't want anyone to find out my intentions too early.

I checked the clock. It was almost seven. I wiped my hands down my navy skirt. It was time.

I took one final glance at my room. It had been my room for so long, and I was leaving it. Maybe when I came back, I wouldn't be here anyway. I would live in the barracks with the knights. The thought brought a smile to my face.

With that, I set off. The trip to the meeting room was much too slow but also too quick. When I got there, Zarios stood outside, leaning against the wall. He was in a pair of maroon trousers and no shirt. It seemed all male minotaurs went shirtless.

I approached, feeling a bit uncomfortable about it all. I was about to announce my engagement. To a minotaur, no less. Though we'd been cordial with them as far as I could recall, I didn't think any human had ever married one, at least not that I was aware of. I could only hope they would go along with it.

He held out his hand. "Ready?" he asked.

I looked down at his long fingers before placing mine between them. "Let's go sell this thing."

He pushed the door open. Everyone was there, Mother, Mama, and Sybil sat on one side of a large desk while Sage sat on the opposite end, filing her nails, ignoring everyone else. Damyr and Kiaza sat on the other side, Kiaza looking over her notes and Damyr looking at Sage in a way I didn't appreciate. Many men looked at her that way, and I'd beaten a few of them up for it. Kendrix stood behind them, and he was the first one to notice us walk in.

His eyes moved down to our joined hands and widened, though he said nothing. I guess the rumor mill hadn't quite made it to him yet. Soon, more eyes were on us, all with some form of interest.

"Sorcha," Mother spoke first. "What's going on?"

I looked to Zarios for a moment, who gestured for me to continue. I cleared my throat. "After some thought, I—we—have decided we want to get engaged."

The silence around us was deafening. I clenched Zarios's hand, hard.

It wasn't broken until Sage started laughing. "You take interest in one guy and want to shack up already?" she asked.

"Shut it," I scowled at her, and she lifted her hands in mock surrender, a smirk still on her lips.

Mother stood. "Zarios, could you excuse us for a moment?"

He looked to me to see what I needed. Though this was all fake, I appreciated the support. I gave a small nod.

Zarios released me. "Of course."

I followed my mothers out of the room, my heart in my throat. We only got to the edge of the hall before

Mother turned. "What are you doing?" she asked. She didn't sound harsh, but she had her typical no-nonsense tone.

I crossed her arms. "We've been spending a lot of time together this past week, and I like him. It seems a minotaur's engagement courting is fairly long, so I want to go with him."

Her gaze bounced around my face that I was sure to keep neutral. If there was one thing I learned from all my time in those damned etiquette classes, it was to never show my true feelings.

"But why?" Mama asked. "I thought you had other aspirations?"

I flinched internally. "They were just a silly dream, it wasn't that serious. And I like Zarios. I think he'll treat me well."

Mama took my hands, her tender gaze almost making me break. "Is he making you?" she asked. "Or is it something else? This seems so rash."

I smiled. "This happens all the time. Didn't you and Mother get married quickly?"

They looked at each other. "Yes, but that was different." Mother said.

"How?" I asked. "Zarios and I like each other. We're of the same class if that was your problem. Is it because he isn't human?"

Mama shook her head quickly. "It's not about that. We just want you to be happy."

"I think he will make me happy." Though I didn't plan to stay with him, something in my tone rang true, even to me.

We all stood in a tense silence. I was all but holding my breath.

"This is truly what you want?" Mama asked.

I squeezed her. "Truly. It feels right."

"It still feels too rushed," Mother said.

I crossed my arms. "Not only is this what I want, but I'm sure it would help things."

"What do you mean?" Mama asked.

"I know what's going on between our nations," I said. I wasn't sure if this would work, but I was going for all or nothing at this point. "I know the magestones went missing, and I know the money we get from that trade does a lot for our nation. A marriage between us could help solidify the trade."

They looked at each other, communicating without words. As a child, I used to ask how they did that, but they always said it was from years of marriage.

"Even if you don't care about how I feel, you have to know this is for the good of everyone." I knew I was pressing all the right buttons, but I wasn't sure if it would be enough.

Mama's eyes got watery. "Of course we care about how you feel."

They did the no talking communication thing once again before Mother sighed. "I accept, then. I know Valcor has their own engagement rituals, but I would appreciate you planning on having your wedding here."

I reached for them both, hugging them tightly. "You have my word."

Mama was fully teary when I pulled away, which I should have expected, but Mother looked faintly pleased. Like I thought, she was probably glad I stopped pursuing the knighthood. I ignored that. When I came back, it would all be different.

We went back to the room. My parents took their place behind the desk, and I stood back with Zarios. "I will allow you to court my daughter," Mother said.

"Thank you," Zarios exhaled, bowing slightly for the first time in the entire trip. His group looked shocked by the action, and so did my Mother.

"On the condition she can return if things don't work out," Mother continued. "And there will be a wedding held here."

"Agreed," he said. "But I plan to make her very happy."

Moons. I had to resist my eye roll. He was really milking it.

"Turning to what we came here to speak about," Mother said, "we would like to continue looking into the issues going on before the next magestone shipment. I know because of the engagement plans that will probably be pushed to the side. Are you in urgent need?"

I squeezed Zarios' hand tightly. Even after an intended union she couldn't be honest? I had to believe she had her reason, but it was baffling to me. And I was slightly upset on his behalf.

Zarios, for his part, didn't show any true reaction. "That would be acceptable. Though we did send payment as negotiated, so no other payment will transfer until we receive the shipment."

"That's fair."

"Do you still plan to leave tomorrow?" Mama asked.

"Yes," I said. "We want to do this as soon as possible."

My mother looked at me one more time, and at my nod, she sighed. "Very well. We will leave you so you can pack."

I nodded and followed Zarios out of the room. The door clicked shut behind us, no one following us out. My hands were shaking, so I held them together behind me.

We took a few steps down the hall before facing each other. Zarios didn't show much emotion, the way he always was. "It worked," I said in disbelief.

"I knew it would," he said casually.

I snorted. Though there was something different about his tone that told me he was also pleased the plan was working. "Whatever. Now what?"

"Now, we prepare for tomorrow and set off early. I want the tour to begin as soon as possible. I'll send word tonight to let everyone know."

I nodded. "See you tomorrow?"

He gave my hand a light squeeze, reminding me we were still holding them. It felt strangely comfortable. "Tomorrow," he confirmed.

Zarios released me, and I turned down the hall towards my rooms, my face ablaze.

About an hour later, there was a knock on my door. When I opened it, Sage stood on the other side. I was surprised, she was normally out at this time. "Can I come in?" she asked.

I held the door open further, letting her pass. "What's up?" I asked.

She looked at my bags. "So you're getting married? I didn't think it would be you." Her laugh was faint.

I sat on the bed. "Me either, but I'm happy."

"Are you?" she asked. "You've never been one to make a quick decision like this."

I crossed my arms. "What do you mean?"

"I guess I'm just wondering...is this for real or another one of your plans?"

"Plans?" I asked.

Her brow quirked. "Since we were children, you've been scheming to get into the knights. I'm sure that's what you're doing now, but I can't figure out how."

She plopped down next to me. "No scheming," I said. "Zarios is kind, and I'd rather him than some other noble I'd be set up with."

Sage scoffed. "You know our mothers wouldn't let that happen."

I shrugged. "You never know, and I just wanted to have this choice." I felt terrible lying to her. Sage and I had always been the rebels, thicker than thieves. Though we did it in very different ways, we were always in on it together. I would help her sneak out to parties and let her back through my window when she returned. She would make excuses to our instructor about why I wasn't in class while I was off training for my practicals. As much as I wanted to tell her, I couldn't risk it. If she told anyone, the whole plan would be ruined. Expecting her to keep a secret that big wasn't fair.

She narrowed her eyes but then shrugged. "Whatever. It would have been nice if you told me earlier, but springing it on me with everyone else was what I deserved, I guess."

I pulled her into a hug. "I'm going to miss you too."

She took a deep breath and hugged me back. "You're coming back, right?" she asked quietly.

"Of course. We already promised to have a wedding here, and when this is all over, you can come to visit me whenever."

She scoffed, pulling away. "You know I hate traveling, but maybe."

Another knock sounded. Sage and I looked at each other, knowing who was there.

I opened the door to find Sybil, still in her dress from the day, her hair neatly tucked behind her head.

"Oh," she said, looking at Sage. "I didn't realize you had company. I can—"

"Come in," I said, pushing open the door.

She looked between us. "I'm sure Sage already grilled you about being certain?"

"More like roasted," I said with a snort.

Sage bumped my shoulder. "I just had to be sure."

Sybil looked at me, all humor gone. "And you are? Sure, that is?"

"Yes," I said without hesitation. Sybil could sniff out a liar anywhere. I needed to be extra careful with her.

"Very well," she said, sitting on the edge of the bed with us. Though she was letting it go, I could tell she still had her doubts. As long as she'd keep it to herself, however, that was fine with me. Her back remained perfectly straight, her ankles crossed. Always so perfect. "It sounds like we should celebrate."

From the satchel on her side, she removed a small packet I recognized anywhere. I snatched it from her hands before she could react. "Are these juneberry candies?" I asked with excitement.

I fished one out and popped it in my mouth. It melted on my tongue, the sweet and sour taste filling my senses. "Where did you get these?" I asked. "They're not in season."

Sybil reached for one of her own before Sage did the same. "Unlike the two of you, I prefer savoring these things. My bag usually lasts until a month before they come back. But I thought since this was a special occasion, they were needed."

I looked at her as if she'd lost her head. "How? They're so good, I suck down a full bag in an hour."

"It's called self-restraint," she said with a smirk.

I rolled my eyes. "Boring," I said as I shoved a few more in my mouth.

"Be nice," she said. "Or else I'll take them back."

She went to reach for them, but my reflexes were faster. I hopped from the bed and moved out of reach.

She gasped. "You little..."

I laughed, running around the room as she chased me. Sybil cornered me, but I sealed the bag and tossed it to Sage before she reached me.

Sage caught it and ran to the other side. It felt like we were children again, Sybil without the weight of the crown looming over her, Sage without her rebellious charm.

Me without an engagement.

I smiled. I wished I could tell them I would be back to stay sooner than she knew, but instead, we spent the time we could together, running around and sharing candy.

Chapter Eight

ZARIOS

The next morning as I walked through the halls, I felt everyone's eyes on me. With the announcement, I knew I would, but it didn't feel any less odd.

Last night, I had managed to slip away to my room before Damyr found me, but I had no such luck with breakfast. "There you are," he said with a grin. "Man of the hour. Come sit."

I joined him, pouring some coffee and sipping it deeply. He smacked my shoulder, almost causing me to spill. "What the hell, man? I'd been seeing you sneak around with that Yulean girl, but mating?"

I set my cup down. "The heart wants what it wants, I guess." I'd heard that saying before and hoped he would accept it and move on.

To my dismay, he didn't. "But a human? I mean, don't get me wrong, those sisters are hot, but they seem so breakable. I'm sure you've already found that out, though, haven't you?"

I reached for the toast and jam, not willing to even pretend to talk about that. Though many minotaurs talked openly about intercourse, and there was nothing wrong with that, I knew humans were more reserved. I wouldn't embarrass Sorcha, fake intended or not.

Kiaza joined us then, saving me from Damyr. "Good morning, sir," she said.

"Good morning. Have preparations been made to depart?"

"Yes," she said, flipping through her notes. "Everything is ready, and messages have been sent to all the Claraks. I hope to have responses by the time we return."

A smile touched my lips thinking of how shocked Naram would be when he found out. That smile quickly faded, though, thinking about how he could be the one betraying me. "Excellent," I said instead, my mouth feeling like sandpaper. "I want to set out from Ashmore in three days."

Her eyes widened. "Three days, sir? That's very quick."

"I know, but we need to get the new magestone shipment scheduled quickly, and that won't happen until our tour is over." I also didn't want to schedule the shipment until we figured out what happened. Though the stones were, for the most part, harmless, they were very expensive and would sell well on the black market. They could be looking for money, and who knew what they would do with it.

She nodded. "I will send someone ahead."

She got up to move, but I clasped her shoulder. "Have breakfast first."

She nodded and blinked, as if she totally forgot that was what she'd come here for. "Right."

With her here, Damyr stopped his pestering, but he still talked, whether anyone was listening or not. It was a true talent of his, yapping without abandon, but I was used to it. He'd always been like this. Even as calves, he was too noisy.

Once we finished, Kiaza went to complete her work, and Damyr and I finished packing. By mid-morning everything was ready. The horses were packed and ready, the carriage set up for Sorcha.

As if on cue, she appeared. She was in a simple cream dress with her hair down around her face. She had a small satchel at her side, and I could see a small dagger hilted on her ankle. We'd spoken about her keeping her sword hidden. It was better if everyone underestimated her.

Her sisters walked her out alongside her mothers. They did make a very sweet family. Though my father was no longer around, my mother lived in Ashmore, and I was sure she would want to meet Sorcha. That was another reason for the quick departure. Though I did want my mother to meet my actual intended, this wasn't real.

Sorcha said her goodbyes to everyone, Elsbeth tearing up. Though I wanted to be on our way, I wouldn't rush them. I was taking their daughter—in their eyes, forever.

When she was done, she approached me.

"Ready?" I asked.

She nodded. Her eyes were red rimmed and a bit watery. I knew even though she was getting something out of this, leaving her family for it was hard. I didn't know what I could say in this situation, so I said nothing. I put my hand on the small of her back and led her away.

I walked to the carriage and opened the door. When she stepped in, I moved to close the door but felt resistance.

"Aren't you coming?" she asked me.

I huffed. "No. I will be riding with everyone else." I knew Kiaza would be angry when she found out, but that would put us in a very close proximity I wasn't sure I could handle right now.

She shifted, stepping back out. "Then I will as well."

I sighed. "It's fine. The ride is long, and our horses are larger than what you're used to. Just ride in the carriage."

She folded her arms across her chest. "I am capable of riding a horse."

"We don't have an extra," I argued. "And loading up one of yours will take too long."

"Then figure it out." My teeth ground in irritation I was careful not to show. Arguing before we even left the castle gates wouldn't look good.

I leaned in close to her. "We need to look happy and in love, remember?"

Her eyes narrowed, wrinkles forming between her brows. "I don't care. I'm not riding in the carriage."

I closed my eyes, rubbing my forehead. Stubborn girl. "Fine. But you have to ride with me."

I could see her surprise, but she wasn't backing down now. "So be it."

We approached my horse, and she gazed up at him. Her eyes widened briefly, and while I thought their ginormous size would be enough to deter her, she threw her foot into the stirrup that almost hit her chest and forced herself up.

She stood easily, but I could tell there was no way she would be able to throw her legs over.

She let out a small cry when I lifted her and placed her on top. She scowled at me, but she said nothing as she settled in. I hopped up behind her, grabbing the reins and getting comfortable. Her back was pressed to my front, despite our shared effort to stay apart. There was just no extra room on the horse.

When everyone was ready, we set out. Sorcha looked back as we left her home behind.

The journey was long and tiresome. We were only halfway through the day, and I was already becoming irritable. Not only did I prefer to ride alone, but having Sorcha this close to me made me...uncomfortable. Her soft body pressed so tightly to mine was distracting, and my cock was not taking the hint, constantly threatening to arise. It didn't help that she continued to wiggle around, unable to sit still. I thanked the moons she was at least quiet.

When the sun was high in the sky, we pulled off to a clearing for lunch. I hopped down before putting my hand out for Sorcha. She ignored it and tried to get down on her own, turning her body towards the horse to shuffle herself off.

She almost made it when her foot caught on the stirrup, and she let go of the horse. Thankfully, I was there, catching her easily as she falls back against me with an oof.

Her gaze met mine, her face tinged with pink. "Thanks," she muttered as I set her down.

"You could have just accepted my help," I said.

"I was fine," she countered.

I rolled my eyes. "Sure."

She walked away, heading towards the stream running on the edge of the clearing.

I helped Damyr unpack our food, simple sandwiches and fruits given to us by the Queens. We stood around eating, all of us needing to stretch our legs.

"You know," Damyr said, "if the princess isn't using the carriage, I wouldn't mind. I'm exhausted."

"Don't even think about it," I said. Kiaza was in there, and I was sure she'd strangle me if I left her alone while Damyr yapped the entire time.

"Why?" Sorcha asked, appearing at my side. "I have no plans on riding in it."

She reached into the bag with the sandwiches and pulled one out. Her face and hands were now damp, as if she'd splashed water on them.

Damyr gestured as if to say 'see,' but I shook my head. "I don't know why," I said. "It's perfectly comfortable."

"And so is the horse," she said between bites.

I had to disagree, but I wouldn't spend time arguing.

Soon, we were rested and back on our way. Luckily, we were able to reach an inn on the outskirts of Valcor before night fell. On the edges sat a wider variety of beings. Though Valcor was considered minotaur country, it was open to anyone, and where borders met, there tended to be a larger mix.

We stepped into the inn filled with patrons, some human, some minotaur, some others, like demons and even a dragon. Damyr and Kiaza went to the counter to grab keys while I put away the horses. Sorcha insisted on helping, and I was too tired to argue.

When we were done, we met Kiaza, who held out two keys.

It quickly dawned on me that we would be expected to stay together. Sorcha seemed to realize it too, but her reaction was so slight, I barely noticed it.

I thanked her and took the key.

Damyr appeared a moment later. "Would you lot like to join me for a drink?" he asked.

"You crazy bastard," I said. "No one wants to drink, and you shouldn't either. We have a long day tomorrow." Not to mention, I always worried when he drank.

"Don't worry," he said. "I'll just have one to relax."

I nodded. He had gotten better, and I needed to stop hovering. "Very well. See you in the morning."

Kiaza said goodnight and dipped into her room, leaving Sorcha and I alone.

Neither of us said anything as we unlocked the door to our room. It was smaller than I remembered on my way here, with a bed large enough for two minotaurs to fit comfortably, a small sofa, and a desk with a chair.

"Well," she said. "This is cozy."

I huffed in amusement. "You could say that."

I set our bags down. "I'm going to grab us food. Any requests?"

She shook her head. "I'm going to shower down the hall."

I nodded and left, the door clicking lightly behind me. I took a single deep breath. I could do this. For my kingdom, I could do this.

I grabbed us two bowls of stew and some fresh water before going back upstairs. I didn't see Damyr anywhere, so it seemed he had stuck to his word and only had a single drink.

After retrieving our bowls of stew, I went back upstairs. Sorcha was back from her shower, brushing her damp hair. She wore a simple silk slip that hit mid-thigh. The neckline was low, making me feel as if I would swallow my own tongue.

"Here," I said, handing her one of the bowls.

"Thank you." She set the brush down and picked up the bowl, devouring it. We ate silently, neither of us knowing what to say.

When we were done, I brought our bowls back and took a shower of my own. When I returned, Sorcha was curled up on the small sofa with one of her dresses under her head acting as a pillow, a sheet wrapped around her.

"What are you doing?" I asked.

She turned to face me. "Sleeping?" she said, confused.

"Why are you sleeping there?"

Her brow cocked. "Because I am much smaller than you and fit on the couch just fine."

Her scrunched legs told me different. For a moment, I thought of offering to share the bed, but that thought made me uneasy. "You take the bed," I insisted.

"Where would you sleep?"

"I would be fine," I insisted.

She scoffed. "I am just fine."

"But—"

"Goodnight," she interrupted, turning her body back to the edge of the couch.

I grumbled my displeasure but went around putting out the lanterns. I laid in bed, staring up at the dark ceiling.

Stubborn princess was my last thought before drifting off.

CHAPTER NINE

SORCHA

I AWOKE THE NEXT morning, stretching my legs over the sofa's edge. Though it wasn't the most comfortable sleep, it was good enough. My body was sore from riding such a large horse all day, but honestly, being able to lean against Zarios made it less difficult.

When I got up, he was sitting on the edge of the bed, sharpening his blade. He looked up at me, his neutral face still a mystery to me. "Morning," he said, his voice rough from sleep.

"Good morning."

"There's porridge on the table," he said. "We should be in Ashmore by lunch, so no need to pack extra food. We'll leave soon."

I nodded, grabbing the bowl. There was a bit of honey and fruit scattered over the top, the same breakfast I ate at home every day. Though we'd seen each other a couple times at breakfast, I was surprised he remembered. I took a bite, savoring the sweetness.

When I was finished, I set my bowl aside and went to the bathroom to change. I freshened up and got dressed before heading back to find Zarios was changed into new pants, though they still hugged his thick thighs so tightly, it looked as if they might burst.

We gathered our things and went downstairs to meet Damyr and Kiaza, who were already there. The horses were out of their stalls, ready to go.

"Good morning, lovebirds," Damyr said as we approached. "Sleep well? Hopefully not much," he added with a waggle of his brows.

"It's too early for you," Zarios said, but it lacked any real anger. It seemed they were closer friends than I initially thought. His attention shifted to me. "Can I convince you to take the carriage?"

"Not a chance."

He let out a huff I was starting to understand to be his irritated one, and I followed him to our horse. He was tall and gray, with darker spots scattered around his coat. I'd been able to ride a horse since I was a child, but these seemed like a different beast all together. Minotaurs were large, so it made sense their horses would be as well, but these were massive. My legs barley dangled on either side. Yesterday I found myself sitting comfortably cross-legged a few times with how wide their backs were. And though it was fairly uncomfortable, it was better than being in the carriage. I didn't want to be seen as the helpless princess who needed to ride in the carriage, even if that's exactly who I was pretending to be.

Zarios helped me up then followed behind me. There was something comforting about his large body surrounding mine. Though I didn't need to be comforted, I could admit it was nice.

The rest of the way to Ashmore was much quicker, though I was even more sore when we started through the larger village surrounding the capital. Their castle itself was very different from Peradona's. It was a dark stone, without any large spires sticking from the tops. It was mostly level, save for the rounded dome that flew a massive Valcor flag from its peak.

When we arrived at the front, there were no servants waiting around to assist. Zarios hopped off the horse and again offered me his hand. I once again ignored him, snaking down the horse myself, careful not to catch my foot this time.

I managed it well enough, flattening my dress as I landed. He shrugged but moved to grab our bags. I tried to help, but he shooed me away. When I argued, he just ignored me, his hooves clicking on the cobblestone as he made his way inside.

I followed after him, having to hold a brisk pace to keep up. The interior was dark, with stone floors and sparsely lit large spaces. It wasn't bleak per se, but it wasn't like Peradona, with the white marble and large windows everywhere.

We walked a bit further before I ran into something hard and warm.

I had been so focused on my surroundings, I hadn't realized he stopped. He turned, and I averted my gaze, mumbling my apologies.

"Tired from the horse, Princess?" he asked.

I glared at him, crossing my arms. "I'm perfectly fine. You should let someone know when you're stopping."

His brow rose under his fringe. "You want me to tell you every turn I take?"

Red flooded my cheeks. "Let's just go," I said, trying to push past him.

As I did, he turned into me, putting his hand above the door, blocking me in. We stood there, his large body looming over me, his dark eyes piercing through me. "What?" I asked, sounding more breathless than I meant to.

"I'm turning to open the door," he said, voice low. "I thought you might want to know."

I smacked him in the chest lightly. His fur was softer than I expected, like a cozy blanket. It reminded me of the fuzzy one Sage kept on her bed, though that was wool.

He smirked, and my heart skipped a beat. We stayed like that for another moment. My breath came up short at his closeness. His gaze was molten until something in them shifted. I wasn't sure what, but it broke the spell, and he opened the door behind me. When I turned, I was shocked to find a cozy looking space. Though the walls were the same dark stone, most of them were covered by large bookshelves, filled to the brim. There was a crackling hearth to the side, along with a few scattered sofas and sitting chairs, multiple doors around the bookshelves.

Zarios set our bags down. "Are these your rooms?" I asked.

"Yes," he said, his tone flatter than before.

"Huh," I said.

"Is it that strange?" He started pulling things from his own bag.

"I just expected more...weaponry."

"I do keep a sword beneath my bed, but weapons aren't my idea of good décor."

He pulled a few files for his bag and headed for the door. "Where are you going?" I asked.

He wouldn't meet my eye. "I have duties to attend to before we leave in a few days."

"Okay," I said. "What do I do?"

It was obvious he hadn't thought about it. "I don't care. You'll probably see Lunar at some point today for measurements, but do whatever you want otherwise."

"Measurements?" I asked.

"Yes. Kiaza mentioned something about preparing outfits for you. I'm not sure."

"Shouldn't we prepare, though?"

"The plan is very straightforward," he said, sounding exasperated. "We don't need planning."

I wanted to argue, but his tone reminded me too much of my mother's when she was about to shut me down. His gaze never met mine, as if he was annoyed simply by my existence. "Fine."

He nodded and left, clicking the door shut behind him. I looked around, trying to figure out what to do next.

I guess if he didn't want to do any planning, I would have to. I perused his shelves of books, knowing one must be helpful. I grabbed a few addressing some basic history and even some fighting technique before settling in.

Though my eyes skimmed the words, my mind fluttered back to our previous conversation in the hall. His closeness made me feel warm all over, but when we got in here, it was like a switch flipped, and he turned cold and distant. I wasn't sure what was going on, but whatever feelings were bubbling within me had to be cast aside. This was my first mission, probably the most important one I'd ever have.

With that thought in mind, I brought my focus back to the words and got working.

CHAPTER TEN

ZARIOS

THE CARAVANS WERE READY for the trip. The procession consisted of guards in the front and back, my needed advisors in different carriages scattered throughout, the grand carriage in the middle meant for me and my intended. It was gaudy and spoke heavily of wealth. I tried to insist on traveling without it, but Kiaza informed me others may take it as a show of disparity to not bring it. It sounded like bullshit to me, but here we were, with the large contraption in the middle.

"All set to go, Grand Clarak," Tashna, one of the guards, informed me.

"Great, thank you."

I looked around for a moment before I saw a short head of hair making her way through the crowd. Sorcha wore a dress obviously made for her by Lunar, the court's seamstress. It was blue, with a short sleeve top and a skirt with two large slits down either side, the same as many other minotaur women.

This is the first time I'd seen her awake in three days. I rose early and snuck out to get work done, only to return by the time she was asleep in one of the other rooms. The other night made me realize I was getting off target.

Closing her against the door the other day had been meant to tease her, but having her that close underneath me sent desire pulsing through my veins. In that moment I thought about dropping to my knees and...

I stopped that line of thought. That couldn't happen. Though we looked intended, we weren't. She would be leaving, and getting attached could cloud my judgment. There was too much at stake for that.

Once she noticed I was looking at her, her face shifted, and she walked towards me. "Ready to go, Princess?" I asked as she approached.

"I would appreciate it if you stopped calling me that," she grumbled.

"I'm sure you would," I said. "Ready?"

"Of course, King Zarios."

It was my turn to scowl. She turned to the large carriage. "We have to ride in that?" she asked.

"We do." I didn't want to either, but we needed to keep up pretenses.

"Great." I opened the door, and she stepped up, settling onto one of the benches. I looked inside, concerned about the small amount of space.

"Coming?" she asked.

I slung my bag over my shoulder and got in. I sat across from her, the carriage creaking under my weight. My legs were so long, I couldn't help but touch her with my knees.

Once we were ready, the troop set out. Our first stop was Sobury. They were closest to the capital and visited frequently. Atalin, their Clarak, was generally kind, but she was very traditional, and that meant she, more often than not, fought against my policy changes. Not when it came to lowering the taxes, or starting different jobs programs throughout the kingdom, but when I tried to change the rule about Grand Claraks being married within the first five years of their reign, I was shot down, and she was a major opponent.

We rode for hours, and I kept my eye out for anything unusual in the forest. Thankfully, I didn't see anything of note. I noticed Sorcha doing the same, her eyes hovering back and forth over the woods.

When the sun hung high in the sky, we stopped in a clearing for lunch. I hopped down and glanced over at Sorcha.

"Need any help?" I asked her. Though the carriage steps weren't that high up for me, but compared to her smaller size they were more difficult.

She glared. "I'm fine."

She stepped out, but as she did, she tripped on her own feet and fell. I stretched my arms out and caught her, her body landing on mine with a thud. Her arms wrapped around my neck, and I grabbed onto her thighs as they fell around me on instinct.

We were face-to-face, her clean, berry smell filling my senses. Her eyes were wide, but she narrowed them quickly. "I was fine," she insisted.

"You were falling," I said with a quirked brow.

"On purpose."

"Right."

We stood there for another few moments, eyes locked. I took in her dark features, her determined jaw, her deep eyes, lost in all that was *Sorcha*.

"Foods up," Damyr said, approaching the two of us.

The moment between us broke, and I put her down. She looked as dazed as I felt, but she quickly righted herself and headed off towards the meal line.

Damyr looked after her. "Looks like you and your mate will be having a good night," he said, waggling his brow.

I only hummed, irritated at him for breaking the moment, though that was ridiculous. There was no moment between us.

We ate quickly and got back on the road. Once the sun was almost set, we arrived in Sobury. It was a larger territory that specialized in agriculture, situated along a river, making the soil perfect. A lot of the food for Valcor came from here, and some was even shipped out of the port in Mertis.

Sorcha's eyes bounced all around, interest clear on her face as we got closer to our destination. "Is this Sobury?" she asked.

"Yes," I confirmed. "Our first territory stop."

"I heard that they had large farmlands, but I didn't expect it to look like this."

I followed her gaze. Though there was a small main town, just beyond it were large fields full of crops. It was fall, so they were full of jarrl fruits growing on thick, winding vines, making the fields look almost wild and untamed.

"I'd read about it a bit, but seeing the vast fields in person…" She trailed off. "They look so different than those in Peradona."

"What book?" I asked her.

Her cheeks tinged a slight pink. "I wanted to do some preparation, so I read up about each territory. There wasn't much, but I found a few of the books helpful."

"Have you left Peradona?" I asked, trying to continue the conversation. Maybe I was trying to make up for ignoring her for three days, but I wouldn't examine the thought too deeply.

"A few times," she said, eyes still glued out the window. "But not much. We do a bit of traveling in the country, but I've only been to Nordin once for a wedding, and Quvill for one of their grand balls Sage dragged me to."

I was slightly surprised she'd been to the kingdom of Quvill. Those were fae lands, and though they were welcoming, they were very secretive. Lots of things there appeared different than they truly were.

"Must have been a big ball if rumors of how the fae party are to be believed."

"They are," she said, waggling her brows.

I laughed as the carriage began to slow.

When I looked out, Sobury's capital building came into view. It was made of solid, dark wood, almost like a giant cabin. Large flower boxes lined the walls, moss crawling up the sides.

Sorcha took the building in with interest. I got the impression there was a lot she hadn't seen, as she had a keen interest in everything.

"Ready?" I asked her.

"As ever."

The large doors opened, and out walked Atalin. She had a cherry-brown coat with white spots and short, dark horns, her hair tied back in braids. She had been around a long time, which always made me shocked when she was so open to certain change. I was sure she would be leaving her position soon, and I would need to host a choosing ceremony. It would be my second after appointing Naram, and I hoped to have this resolved before then.

She was followed by her advisors, as well as her own personal guard. Her mate had passed the previous year, and she'd been a bit different since. "Grand Clarak Zarios," she said, bowing slightly. "We are honored to host you and your intended mate."

"Thank you," I said. "This is my intended, Princess Sorcha Yulean."

I held my arm out, gesturing to her. "So nice to meet you," Atalin said, bowing slightly.

"You as well," Sorcha said, bowing her head to Atalin. A gasp rang out among the surrounding crowd. Sorcha sat up and looked around, trying to figure out what was wrong. My stomach sank. We'd been here for a few minutes, and she was already showing weakness.

Atalin looked at me in confusion. "I apologize," I said. "Sorcha isn't quite accustomed to our ways." I was all but holding my breath, hoping she wouldn't say anything.

Sorcha looked at me in confusion, but I didn't return the glance. I needed to keep everyone's attention on me.

Atalin nodded. "Be sure she learns," she said. "I am much more understanding than the others."

I gave her a single nod, some of the tension leaving me.

"Good," she continued. "Let's head inside. I'm sure you're exhausted from your journey."

Sorcha was still eyeing me as we followed the crowd inside. The interior of the building was almost exclusively made of glass framed by wood, letting natural light illuminate the space. Vines climbed the sides, clinging to the wood. The floor was glass and housed an expansive terrarium underneath, filled with plants native to the area.

Sorcha took in every little detail, her gaze moving around the space quickly.

Atalin made small talk until we were led to our suite of rooms. "This is your room," she said to us. "I'll let you get settled before the feast tonight. Please let one of the servants know if you need anything."

"Thank you," I responded before stepping into the room. Sorcha followed closely behind until the door clicked shut.

"What was that?" she asked, throwing her bag down.

I slouched on the small couch in the room. "Your show of weakness?" I asked. "Unacceptable."

Her eyes widened. "Weakness?"

I nodded. "Bowing to someone symbolizes your defeat to them, your status beneath them. You can't do that. As the Grand Clarak's mate, you must never show weakness."

"In Peradona, it's a sign of respect," she said. "How was I supposed to know it was different here? You never told me."

I sighed. She was right, but I was too stubborn to admit it. My face fell a bit, and my tone softened. "It doesn't matter. Now you know, and it was only Atalin. But she is correct. Some of the others wouldn't take that show of weakness lightly, misunderstanding or not."

"I get it," she snapped. "Anything else I should know before I make an ass of myself once more?"

"Never do anything to show any weakness." I tried to say it as a warning, but she seemed to take it as an insult.

She scoffed. "Yeah, I'll get right on that. Now what do we do?"

"For now, we rest," I said. "I'm sure you're tired from traveling, and we need to be at our best for tonight. Remember our plan."

"I remember," she said defensively. "And I'm not that tired. I'm fine."

"Well, I am," I said. "And you should really try to rest. The best time to do some snooping will be while everyone is at the party, which means we'll probably be up late." I hopped up onto the bed and relaxed back.

At least, I attempted to. Sorcha was pacing around, searching every nook and cranny. "What are you doing now?" I asked.

She turned, as if I caught her doing something wrong. "I'm just looking."

"Well, look quieter."

She huffed before sitting down and pulling out a book I recognized. "The Controlled Art of Fighting," I read from the back of the cover in a questioning tone.

Her gaze met mine over the spine. "Is there an issue?"

"No. It's just one of my favorites. Not everything I say is meant as a slight towards you."

Her gaze caught mine, and something in it softened. "I can tell," she said, her voice much calmer. "There are lots of notes. They're helpful."

I smirked. "Wow, you found something I did helpful."

Her eyes narrowed. "Don't get used to it."

I chuckled, laying back. Truth was, I was tired, and we needed to be prepared for the night.

CHAPTER ELEVEN

SORCHA

I STARED AT MYSELF in the mirror, taking in this odd style of dress. It was a deep green. The top had a single sleeve that went over my shoulder and ended right above my belly button. The skirt was light, with two slits up either side, I assumed to accommodate the minotaur women's larger legs. I preferred it to the Peradonian style of heavy skirts and tight corsets. These were much more lightweight and comfortable.

I braided my hair half back to keep it out of my face before adding the headpieces Lunar had made me. She explained it was normal for minotaur women to decorate their horns for mating ceremonies and made me something to wear. It was a headband that had two horn-like pieces made from silver metal sticking from the top. They were adorned with metallic flowers and other swirly designs made from colorful metals.

I managed to strap my miniature dagger under the waistband of my skirt, hidden seamlessly. Once I was satisfied, I headed out of the bathroom and into the main room. Zarios was now fitted in armor obviously made for show. It was silver and ornate, with intricate filigree surrounding what looked like a crest I recognized from one of the books I picked up. It was akin to a king wearing a crown. Grand Claraks wore this crest to symbolize their position. His fringe still sat over his eyes, hiding any tell of what he was thinking. Over the past week, though, I felt like I could get a better read on him even with his eyes hidden.

He did a lot of huffing, but they were all different. His irritated huff was louder, while when he was amused, it was more of a light puff. He also didn't visibly redden when embarrassed or upset, but I noticed when I corrected one of the notes in his book earlier, his tail swished hard behind him. I had to hold back my laughter when it happened.

When he turned to face me, he paused. I wasn't sure why, he wore an expression I hadn't seen before. It cleared as quickly as it appeared. "Are you prepared for tonight?"

I scoffed. "Of course." Annoyance bled through my tone. I was sick of him underestimating me, of everyone, really.

He assessed me once more then adjusted his bracers. "When we go down, we need to make them believe we're together." He sighed, rubbing his horn. "Minotaurs are...affectionate with their mates."

I could feel my face heat. "What do you mean?" He hadn't mentioned any of this. Was it just hand holding? Kissing? Were we expected to get naked and fuck right on the table?

"Nothing like you appear to be imagining," he said, seeming to sense my thoughts. "They just expect to see physical touch, so keep that in mind."

I nodded, trying to keep my hot face under control. My mama had a reactive blush that was passed to me, and I cursed it often.

"Shall we?" he asked. He didn't wait for a response, he just headed towards the door. I followed, almost running to catch up. It felt like I was running after everyone in this kingdom. Though I was fairly tall for human women, I was much shorter than everyone here.

He comfortably led us through the corridor, telling me he'd been here before. I was sure to keep my guard up.

As we rounded the next corner, I could hear music streaming in down the hall. He stopped and waited for me to approach. When I did, he held out his hand. I hesitated for a moment but placed mine in his. His larger hand enveloped mine almost fully, making my anxiety dissipate a bit.

We took another sharp left, and before we entered the ball room, he leaned in and whispered, "Just stick by me and try to behave."

My eyes narrowed. "As long as you don't forget to tell me anything important," I whispered back sharply.

In the next step, we went from the annoyed allies to a couple who looked like they were in their honeymoon phase. I slapped a smile on my face, letting my gaze relax, and I could feel him do the same. It was almost unnerving how quickly we fell into this charade, but it was all the better for us.

The atmosphere when we entered took my breath away. We had stepped outdoors into the back garden. Beautiful flowers adorned each table, and large bundles of wisteria cascaded down the fences lining it all. I couldn't tell if they were growing there or added for the occasion, but they were beautiful.

We moved to the long, head table in the front. Atalin was there, her horns adorned with leafy greens and twigs that could easily look messy, but she made them look classy. Though she was slighter than most males around her, she held herself in the way someone in charge would. Her dress was similar in shape to mine, with the top and bottom being two pieces and two large slits down the skirt, though hers was much simpler, in a cream color that complimented her cherry-brown and white-spotted coat.

There were others milling around the space, drinking and conversing, but unlike what I was used to, everyone was in simple attire. Though it was all nice, we stuck out with all our extra jewels and color.

"It's great to see you both," Atalin said. "Please, settle for dinner and make yourselves comfortable."

"Thank you for your hospitality," I said kindly, being sure not to bow this time.

She smiled and was off, greeting another pair who'd walked in. It seemed people were beginning to settle in. We did the same, sitting at the head of the massive table. I was worried about needing to mingle with everyone here, but we weren't approached as we were served our dinner.

Drinks came soon after. I took a big swig, and when I put it down, Zarios leaned in. "Don't drink too much," he said. "We need to stay sharp."

"I know that," I gritted quietly through my teeth. I was sick of him acting like I had no idea what I was doing. Like I didn't also have my future on the line.

We were served course after course of food until I was close to bursting. Eventually, dinner was done, and people were back to walking around. The music picked up, and people began moving to the dance floor.

"Would you like to dance?" Zarios asked.

My mind paused. It was a simple question that had an easy enough answer, but something in my brain held me back. Did he want to dance with me because of the plan, or because he wanted to dance with *me*? The answer was obvious, and it shouldn't matter, but I couldn't seem to reason that with myself.

Though it would be silly, I almost said no. But then I saw something in his gaze—something warm, something meaningful that made me agree. I took his hand, and he led me to the dance floor. The music was upbeat as Zarios took my hand in his and wrapped his other around my waist, pulling me close. I had to crane my neck to look up at him.

He led us with ease, swaying us to the beat. "I'm still impressed you're such a good dancer," I said.

"I'm sure there are many things you'd find impressive about me, Princess."

My face heated. "That's one bold assumption. It takes a lot to impress me."

He snorted. We danced through a few more songs. Though I wasn't excited to come out here, I was having fun.

After the last song ended, the music slowed. For this song, Zarios pulled me somehow closer, and we were left to sway easily together. Though he had a lot of metal armor on that was cold to the touch, where there wasn't any, he was warm and soft.

I rested my head against his chest, and he seemed surprised until I whispered, "When should we slip out?"

He brought his head down near my ear. "Soon. We need to be careful. They can't suspect anything."

I nodded against him. Though I could have lifted my head, I stayed where I was. I told myself it was to keep up the illusion, but it was also...nice, in its own way.

When the song ended, I pulled away. "I need to run to the washroom."

He nodded, releasing me. "I will get us more drinks."

I made my way inside and found the washroom. I was washing my hands in the basin when the door opened, and Atalin stepped in.

"Hello," I greeted, careful not to bow.

"I was hoping to find you," she said.

I was surprised but held my neutral face. "Really?"

"Yes. I must admit, I was surprised when Zarios declared his mate-to-be, but you seem to have a spark."

"A spark?" I repeated.

She smiled. "Call it intuition. You seem to be more than just a princess to me."

Did she know? She couldn't. I laughed lightly. "I don't know about that. I was raised as any other royal is."

She hummed, as if unsure. "But why Valcor?"

"I'm sorry?" I asked.

She leaned against the counter. "As second in line, you probably could have married into any royal family you wanted, in any nation. Why this one? Did your parents force you?"

My brows furrowed as anger coursed through me. "No, I wasn't forced. I make my own choices. I didn't choose for the nation. I chose Zarios." For some reason, those words didn't feel like the truth, but they didn't feel entirely like a lie, either.

She smirked slightly, and I suddenly felt like I had passed some kind of test. "I think you'll be good for him," she said finally.

"What does that mean?" I asked. I knew I should keep my mouth shut, but the question seemed to tumble out on its own.

"I'm sure you'll figure it out." With that, she left me standing there, astounded.

Weird.

I shook it off. I needed to keep focused. We had to slip out soon to ensure we had enough time. When I reemerged, Zarios was by the bar. He had a drink, but he made no move to sip on it. Damyr was there with him, laughing loudly. It was obvious he'd had a bit much, but it was a party.

When I came up beside him, Zarios pulled me in. It took me by surprise, but I leaned into him all the same.

"Hello, Princess Sorcha," Damyr greeted. "Nice to see you again."

"Nice to see you as well," I said. "Looks like you're having fun."

He waved his tankard at me. "It is a party, of course. We'll be here all night."

That was good to know.

"If you don't mind," Zarios said, "I'm going to borrow my intended for a few minutes."

His voice took on a meaningful tone, one Damyr picked up on easily. "Oh, of course. Wouldn't want to bother the new couple."

Zarios led me away, his hand on my lower back. He led me to a row of bushes on the outskirts of the party, pushing us against them so we were in the dark corner. "What are you doing?" I asked him.

He leaned in, looking as if he were kissing my neck. "Giving us an easy way out. Follow my lead. But if you don't like something I do, tell me."

I nodded. His hands moved up my bare thighs to where my skirt split. I followed his lead, wrapping my arms around his shoulders. I let out a low laugh, really selling what we were doing. Being this close to him made desire spring through me, heating my lower belly. It was unexpected, but I allowed myself to enjoy it, even for just a moment.

His large hands moved over my body, down my legs, across my middle. When one hand snaked up and grabbed my throat, my mouth turned dry. I hoped he couldn't see my hard blush in the dark. Suddenly, I could feel his hardness against me. I tried not to react. It was a natural thing, and we were on a job. I knew I was getting too wrapped up in his touch, but I couldn't seem to stop. My mind felt torn between the lust I felt and the job I was here to do.

When he bent to whisper into my ear again, I had to suppress a moan. "We can slip into the garden and go around."

I smiled and batted at him like he'd said something naughty. He grabbed my hand and rushed me away, as if he couldn't wait. I was a bit sad this game we were playing was ending, but it was time for the real work to start.

CHAPTER TWELVE

SORCHA

I ROLLED MY DAGGER at my side, waiting for Zarios to finish changing. Though we were tight on time, the metal sounds could draw unwanted attention. When he approached, gone was the intricate armor, and he was left in a tight pair of black trousers that matched his fur and no shirt. It almost allowed me to imagine him naked.

I shook my head. I didn't need my thoughts to drift there. After sneaking through the garden, we went around and through the servants' doors to get back in.

"You remember the plan?" he asked me.

My fists were white at my sides. "No, I totally forgot," I pressed. "I'm just a silly girl along for the ride."

He sighed, and his tone softened. "I don't think that," he said, as if he truly meant it. "We just can't raise suspicion. If anyone discovers our plan, we won't get another chance."

I let my body relax and nodded. He was right, everything was at stake, and we couldn't let it go awry. "I remember. We won't fail."

I saw my determination mirrored in his gaze. We set out into the hall, heading the opposite direction of the party I could still hear in full swing. We should have full access while people thought we were having a mating ritual of our own.

We padded quietly through the halls, careful not to make any noise. Luckily, all the floors were carpeted, probably to be comfortable on hooved feet, and it went a long way to muffle our steps. Though everyone should still have been at the celebration, we didn't want to alert anyone who may have left. I held my skirt high, careful not to trip over myself.

Soon, we were in a smaller hall lined with doors I assumed to be the offices. I followed Zarios until we reached the last one. He gently clicked the door open, and we made our way inside. Once it was closed, I looked around, my eyes adjusting to the dark. It was a simple office, with plants growing on the windowsills and dark wood furniture.

"You start with the filing cabinet," he said in a hushed tone. "I'll check the desk."

We set out to our tasks, looking for anything incriminating. I would be shocked if it was Atalin, she seemed to have respect for Zarios, but it was anyone's guess at this point.

I opened each cabinet and examined them carefully, pulling out anything I thought could be something, financials mostly. If we were right, the person who stole the magestones was probably planning to sell them, so this was the best bet. We planned to take the files back to our room to review them further before returning them in the morning. I checked the desk, going through the drawers, feeling for any false bottoms or hidden compartments, but nothing stood out to me.

Once satisfied, I turned to find Zarios leafing through some papers, stacks set all around him.

"Find anything," I whispered as I approached.

He shook his head. "I pulled the financials, though, just in case."

We each took a stack of files and fled. I got to the door first, checked it was clear outside, and motioned for Zarios to follow. With my training, I was taught to always pay attention to where I was going, making it easy to lead us back towards our rooms.

As we cut through the hall, Zarios placed his large hand on my shoulder, and I froze and looked up at him. His eyes were on the hall before us, and I soon heard it too, footsteps. They were dulled by the carpet but were heavy. We were only a few halls from our room, but we still held the files in front of us.

I was about to ask him what to do when he pressed me up against the wall, body blocking mine. The files were between us, mostly covered by Zarios' large body. His fur was soft against my skin, making me shiver at the contact. His arms wrapped around my middle, shielding the papers from view.

I looked up, and his eyes were pinning me in place, the dark orbs warming me from the inside out. My breath caught as I saw his gaze flick to my lips. I assumed whoever was at the end of the hall would continue down, but I could hear them approach instead.

"Do you trust me?" Zarios leaned in and whispered.

I nodded without much thought.

As I did, he leaned down and pressed his lips to mine. I hadn't been kissed many times, but it had never felt like this. He tasted earthy, like a good cup of tea with a bit of added sweetness, but what I really noticed was how different he felt. The fur on his body, his longer, thinner lips—so different and yet the best sensation.

We held each other impossibly close, my curves pressing into his large, hard body. Though he was fluffy on top, there was nothing fluffy about what was underneath.

As the footsteps closed in, he deepened the kiss, his rougher, larger tongue meeting mine. We were quickly morphing from an innocent kiss to something that felt much different, much more real. Yet, I didn't think about that as I let his tongue explore me, let him dominate this kiss in a way no one had ever done before.

I wished to grab his shoulders and somehow pull him closer, but I had to hold the files between us. Something hard and way-too large poked into my abdomen that made me gasp just thinking about. I knew he would be larger than any human, but I didn't think he would be quite that large. A light snicker sounded as they passed, but I barely heard it over the sound of my own heart.

When he pulled away, I was left breathless. The hot breath from his snout hit me and made my lashes flutter. His eyes shifted as he backed up, taking his files back.

His throat cleared. "There. They just thought we couldn't get to our rooms quick enough."

"Yes, exactly. Good thinking." I said, trying to keep how flustered I felt to myself. He was right. That was just for the sake of the mission, nothing more.

We hurried back to our room without any more distractions. I threw my pile down on the small desk and looked forlorn as Zarios added to it. I was suddenly regretting forgoing sleep earlier in the day. I was so caught up in making this work, I forgot how late we'd be up.

I plopped down in the chair, prepping for a long night. "What should I look for?"

"Odd correspondence, unlabeled movement of money, anything like that," Zarios said, grabbing his own stack and heading to the armchair in the corner.

"Got it."

We spent hours pouring through the documents, careful to keep them in their same order. I could feel my eyes threatening to droop, but I was determined to keep at it. Zarios brought tea at some point, but that wasn't even enough to keep me up.

"Find anything?" Zarios asked.

I jolted, the sound making my once-closed eyes widen. He was smirking at me, knowing I fell asleep, but I refused to acknowledge it.

"Nothing of note," I said, throwing the last file down.

"Why don't you get some sleep? I can finish this."

"I'm fine," I insisted, going for the next one in the pile.

Zarios plopped his hand on top of it, stopping me. "You need your rest. There isn't much left. I'll finish and wake you to put them back. Wouldn't let you miss any of the action."

I scowled. "I don't need you to wake me. I can sleep when we're done."

I yanked on the file, and it tore free. He shrugged, grabbing the next and leaning back in his chair.

My eyes moved to the single bed on the far wall. It was large enough for the two of us for sure, but we obviously wouldn't share it.

"I'll take the lounge chair," I thought.

"No, you can sleep in the bed," he said easily, his eyes never leaving the pages.

I blinked, unaware I'd voiced that aloud. "You're far too big for the lounge," I said, flipping through the invoices. "I'll be fine."

He gave an irritated huff and whispered something under his breath I didn't catch. I smirked to myself and settled in, glad to have won that sparring match.

All too soon, however, the words on the page turned to drivel, and I drifted off too soon.

Chapter Thirteen

ZARIOS

Sorcha snored softly in the chair across from me, paper strewn about her lap. I picked them up and organized them before adding them back to the pile. I worried her exhausted brain may have missed something.

She was such a stubborn woman. I insisted she sleep earlier because I knew this would happen, but she disagreed. Normally, I wouldn't tolerate such disrespect, but something about her made me relent easily.

As I continued reading through correspondence about the latest wheat harvest, my mind drifted to the hall. I had pulled her to me in an attempt to distract whoever was walking by, and while it accomplished that, I didn't expect the desire that arose within me. Her body pressed to mine with only those files between us... I wished to throw them away, so nothing separated us.

Her lips were so soft and small, a fact I forgot with her large attitude. I wanted nothing more than to press her into the wall and rut into her, potentially tie her up, see that beautiful rope against her skin.

My cock came to life once again, but I needed to stop. This was not a true mating. We were both here on a job, one she was being professional about, and I needed to be the same—no matter how much it felt like that kiss meant something to her as well.

I couldn't continue like this. I shut the file and checked to make sure she was still sound asleep. She was curled in the chair, her hair partially covering her face. Every time she exhaled, one of the pieces flew forward.

With that assurance, I went to the bathroom and turned on the shower, activating the magestones used to heat it.

I undressed and stepped in, my hand quickly going to my cock. I took the blunt tip and stroked it slowly. I imagined Sorcha with me in the shower, her tits that were so pushed up in her dress now exposed and her delicious ass on display.

She would get on her knees for me, but not before she talked back to me. I would fill her smart mouth with my cock until she was gagging on it, until she was so turned on she was playing with herself below me.

Then, I would lift her and eat that juicy pussy until she came all over me, and I would continue even after she begged me to stop, lapping up all her juices greedily. I picked up the pace, working my full length, pulling on the piercing that sat underneath the tip.

My imagination shifted to pushing her against the wall and sheathing my full length inside. I just knew she would feel amazing. She would bounce on my cock until I came deep inside her, until she was so full, there was no way she wasn't pregnant with my younglings.

At that thought, my cock spilled, coating the wall in front of me in thick, white cum. I pressed my head to the wall, careful not to bump my horns and let the water beat down on my back.

That was the hardest I'd ever come, and that was from fantasy alone. I washed the wall then myself. This couldn't happen again. I needed to draw a clear line. We were business partners, if that. This was about mutual benefit, and when it was over, we would part ways. Everything would go back to normal.

When I finished, I dried myself and went back out to find Sorcha was still sleeping in the chair. I picked her up and moved her to the bed, trying not to think about how good she felt in my arms.

I put her under the blanket before going back to my files.

The sun was beginning to shine when I grabbed the documents and headed back to the offices. I knew Sorcha would be upset about not bringing the files back with me, but she looked so peaceful in her sleep, I couldn't bring myself to wake her.

The party was sure to have lasted all night, so I didn't expect anyone to be up, but I still made an effort to be scarce. I put them all away and slipped out without being noticed. As I walked back, I saw Atalin strolling through the garden. She noticed me standing there and gestured me over.

I joined her on the bench, admiring the vast plant life surrounding us. Unlike the neatly trimmed and organized gardens of Peradona, these ones were teaming with a more wild life. Though there were cleared walkways, the flora grew where it wanted. Flowers were mixed in all the beds, and even plants people considered weeds grew, living in harmony with the others.

"I expected you to be too exhausted from your mating to be up this early," Atalin said with a smile.

I huffed in amusement. "Who says I've been to sleep?" That was true, but not for the reason she thought.

She laughed before sobering. "A human is an interesting choice. Do you think she's ready for the trial?"

I stilled. I hadn't thought about that. The Grand Clarak's mate was expected to face a similar physical challenge to the one I faced to become Grand Clarak. "I hadn't planned on holding one." It was honest. Not only did I not plan on it because the engagement wasn't real, but it was a silly ritual.

Her eyes widened. "I don't think that's a good idea. It's important to show to everyone the strength of your mate. I think Prator would agree."

I sighed. Those two were still stuck in their old ways. Their representatives on my council made progress hard for me at every turn, and though Naram tended to be pro change, he went with the tide. He didn't normally fight too hard for it.

Though this worry was for nothing. As soon as we figured out what was going on, we would go our separate ways. So why did the thought leave me feeling...displeased?

"I will figure it out," I told her.

She seemed to accept that answer. "Once this is over, I plan to retire."

I nodded. "I will hold the clan leader ritual whenever you are prepared. Do you have any prospects?"

"There are a few," she agreed. "But there is one I have my eye on. She has the head for it."

"I hope one day, I can make that matter more than physical strength." The clan leader trials had almost nothing to do with intelligence and everything to do with strength. While it was up to the current leader to put up their challengers—and I trusted Atalin to put up people who were ready—that wasn't always the case. It made nepotism too easy, and it needed to be dealt with.

She patted my shoulder. "I hope so too, though I don't expect to live to see it." In that, we seemed to be on the same page.

I huffed. "You have a long while left."

She stood. "I'm sure you'd rather be in bed with your mate than talking with an old woman," she smiled. "Enjoy yourself. Though I know you hate these silly rituals, it gives you a chance to spend lots of time with your mate. Don't waste a minute."

Her words sat with me as I walked back to our room. They sat with me as I prepared to rest for a few more hours. And they sat with me long after I drifted to sleep.

Chapter Fourteen
SORCHA

I TUMBLED BETWEEN THE soft sheets and sighed. It felt nice being able to stretch out across the large bed.

Wait.

I sat up and looked around. I was in a large bed. The large bed in the room I shared with Zarios. How did I get here? When did I fall asleep? I remembered looking through a set of invoices for grain.

Oh no. Was he able to finish? Did he return the files? I threw the blanket off, worried he was in trouble, when the door clicked open.

I turned to see Zarios carrying two trays in his hands. His eyes landed on mine, and the same heat from the night before returned.

"Morning," he said with a slight huff. "I brought breakfast."

"Thank you," I said as he set them down on the small tables the files were no longer sitting on. The same oats, berries, and honey sat in my bowl. Though some of the fruits were different from the ones I had normally, they still looked delicious. It was a small gesture, but every time he brought me breakfast, heat rose to my cheeks.

"Did you find anything last night?" I asked, sitting in the chair across to join him. I picked up the bowl and took a bite. One of the berries popped in my mouth, and the sweet juice exploded on my tongue. I would have to ask him what these fruits were later.

"No," he said, sounding almost relieved.

I waited for him to tell me more, but he didn't continue. I huffed. "Did you get them back without anyone noticing?"

"Of course," he said with an eye roll.

I narrowed my gaze. "I apologize for inquiring about a mission I'm a part of. It wouldn't be good for either of us if you got caught."

He looked to contemplate my words, his expression softening. "You're right. I'm sorry. I'm not used to doing these things with others. I'll be more conscious of it in the future."

I hadn't expected that from him. Though this man could be a grumpy asshole, he did seem to be sincere. "It's fine," I sighed. "Just try not to be an ass all the time."

He smirked. "An ass. Is that a donkey joke?"

I giggled at that, almost spitting my coffee in the process. "No. Just an observation."

I walked to our suitcases to grab my clothes, eager to get out of the dress from the night before, and headed for the bathroom.

Once I was showered and dressed, now in more comfortable loose pants and a t-shirt, I stepped out. Zarios was still there, looking over more paperwork. I assumed it wasn't one we found the night before, based on the Ashmore crest on the front.

"So, what now?" I asked as I approached.

"Now, we perform the mating ceremony and head to Mertis." He stood and stretched his arms over his head, his large chest sticking out even further.

I had to turn to hide my blush. "Anything I should know for this ceremony?"

"I don't think so. Just follow my lead and you should be fine."

I scoffed. "Because that has worked so well so far."

We finished getting ready to go, and I stared at my dresses in disdain. I had no interest in putting it back on.

"What's wrong?" Zarios asked from behind, startling me from my thoughts.

"Nothing," I snapped quickly. I didn't need him to tell me I was being ridiculous, as everyone else had. I didn't mind dresses on occasion, but the fact it was a requirement, one only expected of women, drove me mad.

He quirked his brow and looked to the dress in my hands. "Are you changing?" he asked.

"I'm expected to," I said bitterly.

His head cocked in confusion. "By whom?"

"Everyone," I said, his confusion matched. "Women wear dresses out. That's how it is. Even here, women wear them."

"By choice," he cut in. "Many women here wear them because not only are they stylish, but the double slits make them more comfortable. This nation may need a lot of changes, but women's clothing expectations thankfully isn't one of them."

"Oh," I said. "I was unaware. So I can wear this?" I asked, gesturing to my current attire.

"I do not care," he said. "I would prefer you dress up for the balls, but that's merely for appearances."

"So what—I could just show up naked?" I joked. I folded my dress and tucked it back into my bag.

I turned, realizing he wasn't saying anything, and I was caught in his heated gaze. It reminded me of the one he gave me the night before when he kissed me, as if he was imagining me...

I cleared my throat, and it seemed to snap him out of whatever he was thinking. "As I said, wear whatever you'd like." His voice was rough. He turned away quickly, his tail swishing behind him in small, quick motions.

I put my hand over my mouth to cover my amused laugh, but I was sure he heard it anyway.

We walked to the back garden hand-in-hand, and it looked almost like a wedding was set up. People stood on either side, forming an aisle, Atalin standing at the end, looking as regal as she did the night before.

Even though I'd kept my pants on, I'd still put on the make-shift horns and braided my hair around them. I paused as we approached. I'd been surprised by many things coming here, and I wanted to make sure a surprise wedding wasn't in the plans.

Zarios looked to me when I stopped. I gestured for him to lean in, and he did. "Is this a wedding?" I asked in a whisper. "Because I didn't agree to get married."

He let out his amused huff. "No, Princess. This is just the acceptance ceremony. Every clan leader needs to approve of our union before we move forward. That's what the visits are about."

My eyes widened. "What if they reject me?"

"That won't happen," he said with certainty. "And if it does, I will handle it."

That didn't make me feel confident. Though this was just for show, I didn't want anything more to complicate it. There was enough going on without the added stress.

I needed to do this. I needed to prove myself—not just to these people, but to my parents. When I went home, I would be a hero, one who couldn't be pushed to the side under the guise of my safety. Maybe I could even run my own battalion.

I rolled my neck to recenter myself, the way I did in training, and faced forward. I continued my stride towards Atalin, sure to keep my head high. If this visit taught me anything, it was that minotaurs valued strength, and while

I was in no way stronger than them physically, I could show it in other ways.

By the time we reached the end, I was exuding confidence. My back was straight, shoulders relaxed. I was truly feeling the confidence I was faking, and Zarios' hand in mine definitely helped.

"We welcome Grand Clarak Zarios of Ashmore and his intended, Princess Sorcha Yulean of Peradona." She motioned to each of us. "It has been an honor to have you here," she continued, "and now, I must impart my ruling."

She paused, and it felt like the audience was watching with bated breath. Her gaze traveled to me, and I stood a bit straighter, meeting her eye. She gave a slight smirk before she said, "I accept Sorcha Yulean as the mate of Grand Clarak Zarios. May your union be long and prosperous."

The crowd cheered, and I let out a sigh of relief. When I looked to Zarios, he appeared more relaxed in his own small way. "Thank you, Atalin," he said with a warmth in his voice I'd never heard.

She smiled, patting his cheek. "I wish you nothing but happiness, and I think you've found it."

Her gaze found mine, and for the first time, I didn't hold it, shifting on my feet.

"Well, you best be off," she said. "I wish you luck in Mertis. Remember, if you give Naram enough drink, he will agree to almost anything."

I laughed at that, and to my further shock, so did Zarios. It was a low chuckle that rattled my bones. The sound was lovely, and I wished to hear more.

CHAPTER FIFTEEN

ZARIOS

WE LOADED UP AND readied to head out. The carriage was prepared as it was before, and we were loaded into it like cattle. I again felt too close to her, but somehow not close enough. That kiss had been replaying in my mind since last night, and the proximity made it almost impossible to stop the thoughts.

"How long does it take to get to Mertis?" she asked.

"This will take us two days," I said, irritation bleeding into my tone. I didn't want to be stuck in this cramped thing for two days. "We will stop at another inn before arriving there tomorrow. They're on the coast, so travel will take a bit longer."

Her eyes lit up when I said that. "The coast? That's exciting. I haven't been to the ocean since I was a child."

"Really?" I asked.

She nodded. "We took a trip once when I was so young I barely remember it. The ocean is very far from the capital, and for some reason, my mothers were anxious to take us back."

Her statement reminded me how untraveled she was. It made me think about the things we could do in Mertis.

Though we were there for a reason, we would probably have a bit of down time we could use for exploring.

We moved through the woods efficiently. Luckily, we were having good weather and had been able to make good time. Sorcha fell asleep about an hour in, and I couldn't help but gaze at her longer than necessary.

A few hours in, we stopped for lunch. Kiaza found me as soon as we stopped with updates from Ashmore. It seemed everything was going well. This was the first time I'd been gone for an extended period of time, so I was a bit anxious. There had also been no new reported attacks. Though I was glad for that, it made me nervous that something else was being planned.

Once that was through, I ate a bowl of the stew and bread and I spotted Damyr chatting with some of the knights enjoying their lunches. He made a great general, he cared about those ranked lower than him, brought me issues to keep the battalions happy, and looked out for everyone. It made him a great friend to have on my team.

As I continued scanning the crowd, I caught Sorcha's boot on the other side of the carriage. I snuck up behind her and realized she was shining her dagger out of view of the others. I'd been feeling caught up in my feelings lately, and I knew the perfect way to remedy that.

I walked over, looming over her without even a glance up. "You know, Princess," I said, startling her from her thoughts, "a good knight is always aware of their surroundings."

Her scowl was cuter than I'd ever admit. "Don't think your men are capable?" she asked, tucking it back into her boot.

"They are plenty. I'm just making a point."

"It's a silly one."

"Maybe some practice would help," I said.

She looked up at me, squinting at the sun outlining my frame. "You'd like to practice here?" she asked. "Where?"

"Follow my lead," I said. I held my hand out, and she took it easily. I pulled her up and to me. She followed suit and jumped into my arms. Though I wasn't expecting it, I caught her easily, cradling her body close. She caught onto my plan, nuzzling into my neck to the sound of cheers and whistles around us. Her touch was so warm and soft, one I'd began to crave.

I regained focus and carried her through the woods until we found a clearing, where I set her down and pulled her sword from my second sheath. "That should buy us some time," I said, voice hoarse.

"I would think so, just as long as no one comes to watch," she joked.

I knew no one would dare disrespect their Grand Clarak like that, but the thought of anyone seeing her naked made my blood boil.

"You okay over there?" she asked.

"Fine," I clipped. "Why?"

"You're just doing your irritated swish."

I blinked, trying to parse her meaning. "Irritated swish?" I parroted.

"Your tail," she said. "That's the way you move it when you're upset."

I scoffed. "You're mistaken."

She rolled her eyes. "Whatever you say." She must be lying, there's no way I do that.

Did I do that? I'd always been told I was hard to read, emotionless, a quality that made me a good Grand Clarak, but it seemed Sorcha could read me like a book.

She took her sword and turned it in her hands, getting herself comfortable with it again. I pulled mine from my back. The dark amberstine metal shone in the light. This was the sword my father gave me once I was large enough to wield it, and I'd carried it ever since.

"Some simple sparring? Careful of limbs since we're using real blades," she asked, shifting her feet to stand in a readied position.

"Bring it on, Princess."

We circled each other, trying to read the other's moves. Most minotaurs would swing first, relying on their brute strength in combat. Sorcha took a more thoughtful approach that made her a worthy opponent.

I took a few lazy swings, and she blocked them easily, returning the movements, warming us both up. After a few minutes, she went for a more deliberate swing to my side. I blocked it, but, unwilling to stay on defense, I attacked right back.

Then, the fight began in earnest. We traded blows evenly, neither of us quite gaining the upper hand. The sound of our clinking swords and the life in the forest were the only ones around us.

When sparring, it felt like the weight I carried was lifted from me, and for a few moments, I felt free, especially when I had such a competent opponent.

She faked a side swing and instead lunged towards me in the middle. I barely had time to block, noticing my off balanced response, she instantly swung again.

I knew she would move that way and dodged her, rolling my foot down and swinging her legs out from beneath her.

I pinned her quickly, knocking her sword away. We laid there for a moment, panting with exhaustion. Her cheeks were beautifully flushed, her arms held above her head.

"I think we've been here before," I said with a smirk.

Being pressed to her like this would never get old. Her eyes were wide, her lips slightly parted. Having her splayed under me like this had my thoughts turning back to the shower. The images I had back then flashed through my mind, each one dirtier than the last.

She huffed. "One day, I will throw you on your ass," she promised. She was breathless and flushed, and I wished it was for a different reason entirely.

"I look forward to it, Princess."

CHAPTER SIXTEEN

SORCHA

AFTER LUNCH, WE WERE back in the carriage, being carted off to Mertis. That sparring round had my blood pumping, making me realize how much I'd missed it in this past week. It also made me rusty, which was the excuse I gave myself for not winning. It was so frustrating—I couldn't even blame it on his strength. He was swift and well-trained, his technique almost flawless. Though I sort of hated him for it, I also found it very attractive. The feeling was confusing, but one I couldn't focus on while we were stuck in this small carriage.

The ride passed with little fanfare. I was always on the lookout for any of the thieves on the road, but it had been mostly quiet. I also enjoyed seeing Valcor. Every small village we rode through was vastly different from Peradona. The buildings were more spread out, seemingly built with the land in mind as opposed to against it.

Once we reached the inn, I could swear I smelled the sea air. It was probably in my head, but it made me excited either way. I helped put all the horses away while Zarios brought our things to our room. Tonight, we opted to have dinner in the tavern downstairs. It was a fairly quiet tavern, with a large bar and wooden furniture. We ate and drank, joined by Damyr and Kiaza.

It was nice getting to know them. Kiaza told me about her parents in Mertis, who she was planning to visit while we were there. Damyr was funny and very talkative. It seemed he and Zarios had a good friendship. Though Zarios pretended to be annoyed any time Damyr opened his mouth, I could tell it was for show.

It even felt like I was seeing a new side of Zarios. Though he was his normal, aloof self, Damyr managed to get him laughing a few times.

"Did he tell you about the time we jumped into the fountain in Raatan?" Damyr asked.

I almost spit my ale. Zarios narrowed his gaze. "Don't you dare."

"Oh, please tell," I said at the same time.

Damyr smirked into his glass. "So, we had just left a wild party, and this one," he said, poking the side of Zarios's cheek. He batted him away before Damyr continued. "had a bad competitive streak back then."

I laughed. "Had?"

Zarios bumped me lightly as Damyr kept going. "Naram bet him that he could beat him in a game of cards, looser had to take a dive in the fountain. Of course, I joined in on the bet and won. They demanded a rematch, which they also lost, and before they both knew what hit them they were running *naked* from the guard, dripping wet in the middle of winter."

I was laughing so hard by the end, I could hardly breathe. Even Kiaza was giggling lightly.

"It's not that funny," Zarios grumbled, his arms crossed and his tail flicking behind him.

"It's pretty funny," I said, wiping a tear from my eye.

"Well, I think I'm going to retire for the night," Kiaza said, standing and stretching. "We need to be prepared for tomorrow." "I'll join you," Damyr said.

She quirked her brow. "Not like that," he said. "Unless..." He winked at her.

"In your dreams," she said before they both left.

"Are you ready to go?" Zarios asked.

"Not quite," I said. "We've been cooped up all day. It's nice to be out. But if you're tired, I can meet you upstairs."

"I can stay," he said. "We're having fun."

Hearing him say that sent the butterflies in my stomach fluttering. There was no one here to perform for, he could have decided to go to bed, but he wanted to stay.

I smiled at him, and to my surprise, he smiled back. "Want to make a bet of our own?" I asked.

He huffed. "I can assure you, I will not be stripping tonight."

I couldn't help my gaze lowering over him, thinking about that possibility. I was blaming my lowered inhibitions on the drinks. "I was more thinking winner has to tell the loser a secret."

"A secret?"

I nodded.

He looked to contemplate it. "Fine. What are we betting on?"

I looked around. "Darts," I said, pointing to the board in the corner.

He chuckled. "You're going down, Princess."

"We'll see." I'd been practicing my knife throwing lately and felt confident about this.

He grabbed the darts from the board and handed me my set. I went first and hit bullseye once, then the inner circle with the other two. When it was his turn, he hit the exact same way, a bullseye and two in the inner circle.

We continued taking turns, our scores almost the same until he slipped up and hit the twenty. "Uh-oh," I drawled. "Someone messed up."

"Don't worry about me," he said, pulling his darts from the board.

We played a few more rounds without him catching back up. I was on my last one. If I nailed this, I would win. I lined up and hit my first bullseye with ease, then my second. I was about to throw the third when someone coughed directly behind me. I jumped and threw my dart to the side, hitting the eleven.

I gasped and turned around. Zarios was standing a step behind me, looking in his ale as if nothing happened. "Cheater!" I accused.

"I have no idea what you're talking about," he said nonchalantly. "Go get your darts."

I grumbled as I moved to the board and pulled my darts out. He went next and hit the center three times, winning the game.

"You only won because you cheated," I said with a pout.

"I only used what I had to my advantage."

I scowled. "That's just another way to say you cheated." He approached me and ran his finger between my eyes, smoothing the crinkles there. "Don't be mad, Princess. It's just a game."

I wanted to be mad, but his nearness shoved my other feelings to the side. "Fine, but I want a secret too. I should have won."

He gave a huff between annoyed and amused. "Fine. A secret for a secret. I need to think on mine."

"I do too." I didn't have many secrets. What would I tell him? With that, we paid and went upstairs. As we reached the door, Zarios looked at me a little shyly. "Oh, there's something I forgot to tell you."

"What?"

As the door pushed open, I didn't need him to tell me. The room was bare, save for a single bed in the corner and a bedside table on each side. There wasn't even room for anything else. My eyes widened.

"There's only a single bed."

I gulped. "I see that."

"What would you like to do?" he asked. "I can get another room."

"No," I said, too quickly. "We don't want to be suspicious," I quickly amended.

"That means we would need to sleep...together," he said.

I nodded. "That's fine. We're adults. We can sleep in the same bed."

He gave his own nod. We quietly prepared for bed, taking our turns in the shower down the hall until we were both finally ready.

I tried to be normal as I climbed into the right side.

"That's my side," Zarios said as I sat down.

I looked up at him. "Does it matter?"

"Yes. I sleep closer to the door." His face was completely serious.

"I am perfectly capable of sleeping near the door."

"Just let me sleep there," he said, sounding exasperated.

"Moons, if it's such a big deal." I shifted over to the other side and felt the bed sink as his large body got in. My stomach swam with nerves, nerves I tried to let go. What I said earlier was true. We were two adults on a mission, perfectly capable of sleeping next to each other.

That thought left me when I turned and found myself face-to-face with Zarios. The lights were off, so I could barely see him, but his eyes shone in the moonlight. I took in a sharp breath as my lower belly heated.

"Goodnight," I managed. I rolled over, needing to pretend he wasn't right there.

I listened to him shuffle around next to me as I willed myself to go to sleep, though it didn't seem to be happening.

"Princess?" I heard softly.

"Sorcha," I corrected.

"I think I'd like to tell you my secret now."

I turned until we were face to face once again. Now that it had been dark a while, I was able to make out his expression a bit more. His face was serious, his eyes intense.

"Yes?" I whispered.

"I liked kissing you last night."

I felt frozen in time. "You did?"

He nodded.

"I did too," I admitted.

"Was that your secret?" he asked. The intensity in his gaze was the only reason I was honest.

I shook my head. "But I would like to tell you now."

It felt like all the air in the room was sucked away, and I could barely believe what I was about to say. "Tell me," he said lowly.

My mouth felt like sandpaper, my hands sweating. Somehow, he'd gotten even closer.

When I worked up the courage, I finally said, "I'd like to do it again."

A beat passed between us, then another. His face remained the same. I thought about running away. It would be less embarrassing than whatever was happening now.

Before I could formulate an escape plan, I was being pulled forward until I was flush with Zarios, and my hands instinctively went to his chest.

"Are you sure?" he whispered against my lips. He was only a breath away.

I didn't answer. I couldn't. I pressed forward, bringing our lips together. He felt just as good as last time. His warm breath fluttered on my face as he pulled me impossibly close. My hands worked up his shoulders, wrapping around his neck. He had that same sweet tea taste as earlier, paired with the ale we'd had downstairs.

I licked his lips, and his mouth opened, his tongue exploring my mouth however he wanted. His hands came around my hips, gripping my ass hard. I moaned into his mouth, the slight pain turning into pleasure. I could feel how soaked I was from just this kiss. I wanted more.

His hard length poked into my abdomen, and he rutted lightly against me, looking for his own friction. I could feel something else, something hard going along the underside of his cock that I hadn't noticed before. I wondered what it was.

Before that thought could go much further, his hand wrapped around my front, gripping my breast through my slip. He swallowed my sounds of pleasure with his mouth as he flicked my nipple until it hardened. He gave the other one the same treatment, and I pushed against him, finding the friction I craved against his massive thigh.

His mouth moved down to my neck, kissing down my jaw and under my ear.

"Please," I moaned.

He growled, the sound vibrating the whole room. "Do you need to come, Princess?"

"Yes," I cried. I couldn't even play coy. I needed it like I needed my next breath.

He rumbled in approval. My slip was moved up and away, leaving me bare beneath him, save for my underwear. He backed up a bit to look between us, his gaze roaming my body like a caress, heating my entire body.

"Moons, you're gorgeous." His voice was almost reverent. I had to be blushing from head to toe, and I hoped he couldn't tell in the dark.

His mouth came down on my nipple, licking along the hardened bud. My back arched into his touch seemingly on its own, needing to be closer. His body was so warm, it felt as if I would be set on fire by his touch.

Large hands traveled down my body, over my sides and down my stomach, towards the edge of my panties. I shivered under his touch as his finger ran along the seam, down my thigh.

"Can I?" he asked, his voice rough.

"Yes," I said like a plea.

CHAPTER SEVENTEEN

ZARIOS

I DIDN'T KNOW HOW we ended up here. Well, I did. It felt like an inevitability. My lust for her had been simmering just below the surface, waiting to break free. Our passive flirting had moved from an act to something we did without anyone else around.

At the time, I wasn't sure why I'd said it, but now, I realized it was because I needed this. I needed to touch her. I wouldn't last a whole night next to her *without* touching her. I needed to know she felt the same.

This was probably for the best anyway. There had obviously been something going on between us, and ignoring it was a distraction. Maybe getting it out of our system was what we needed.

But now that I had her, naked and sprawled out beneath me, I wasn't sure if I could let her go.

That was a problem for later.

She granted me permission, so I pulled on her underwear until the edges tore and the scraps fell from her body. Her gasp was so cute, I leaned down and covered it with a kiss.

When I pulled back, my eyes were drawn to the apex between her thighs. Her cunt was glistening, a small bit of hair right above a nub I was unfamiliar with.

I ran my finger over it, and she shivered. Interesting. This time, I allowed my finger to circle it, revealing a small bit of skin underneath. I touched it directly, and she moaned loudly, moving her hips to ride against my touch.

"What is this?" I asked, running my finger over it and circling it once again.

She sat up on her forearms to look at me. "What?"

I ran my finger over it again, and her head fell back. "This. What is it? Minotaur females don't have it."

"It's my clit," she said shyly.

"Clit," I repeated, circling. The way she leaned into my touch spurred me on. "It's very sensitive."

She didn't respond, too focused on her pleasure. Wanting to give her what she needed, I continued circling her, trying to use her cues to figure out what felt good.

Soon, my fingers snaked down towards her opening. She was dripping, her scent filling the room. I couldn't help it, I dipped my finger into her tight opening once and drew it to my lips, tasting her sweet, musky flavor.

Moons, it was delicious, and I needed more.

She gasped as I lifted her legs and held them apart, exposing her to me completely. I used one hand to spread her cunt wide between my fingers, just wanting to look at its perfection.

"Zarios," she moaned. "Please."

As much as I wanted to play with her, I craved her as much as she craved release. I brought my face down and ran my tongue along her pussy, tasting her fully. I licked from her entrance to her clit, swirling my tongue around it.

Her hands gripped my horns tightly, trying to move me where she needed me most. Touching a minotaur's horns was a fairly taboo thing outside of a relationship. No one I'd ever hooked up with even attempted it. I knew I could ask her to move her hands and she would, but I found I didn't want to.

I let her guide me, wanting to learn what she liked. She kept my tongue at her clit, and I continued rounding it before lapping a couple of strokes then starting the process over. She wriggled beneath me as I put two fingers to her opening and worked them in, stretching her around my digits. She was going to need a lot of stretching to fit my cock.

"I'm so close," she breathed, so I kept going, forcing her closer and closer to the edge.

"Come for me, Princess," I said against her. "Give all your pleasure to me."

I sucked on her clit hard and felt her walls clench down on my fingers as wetness poured from her, coating my fingers.

Once she relaxed, I let go, pulling my fingers from her. My hand was coated in her slick, and I had the perfect use for it.

I pulled my cock out of my pants and used her cum to lube my cock, running my hand across it. Her eyes caught my movement, and she watched me with keen interest.

I'd never enjoyed having an audience, but something about this made the base of my spine tingle. Her tits bounced with her heavy breathing, and I reached a hand down to play with myself absentmindedly.

A slight whine left her lips, but she just continued to watch as I moved.

I let my touch roll the piercing under my tip, and she looked closer. "Is that…"

"A piercing?" I finished for her. "Yes."Her eyes blew wide. "Can I?" she asked, gesturing towards my cock.

"Please," I said roughly. I craved her touch, but I didn't want her to feel like she owed me anything. "If you want."

She took my cock from my hand, and I groaned at her touch. Her hand was soft and warm, so small against my cock. Her fingers couldn't touch all the way around. She gripped my ridge tightly, and I tensed. It was going to be embarrassing how quickly I was going to finish.

"There's one here too," she observed, pressing on the piercing along my ridge. I hissed, the feeling making my balls pull up slightly.

Sorcha sat up fully and put both her hands on me, playing with my tip and jerking her other hand over my ridge.

"Fuck, Princess. Your touch is magical." She was so pretty beneath me, looking up at me through her thick, dark lashes.

Her mouth fell open at my words, her blush somehow getting deeper. A few thrusts later, and my balls pulled up as I came, fast and hard.

It poured from my tip, covering her neck and tits. She continued to work my length through my orgasm, wringing out the last drop. That final shot hit her open mouth, falling right across her tongue. Watching that made me begin to harden all over again, especially when she closed her mouth and licked her lips.

Moons, this woman was going to be the death of me. I ran my finger though my cum covering her chest and brought it to her lips.

"Open," I commanded.

She did without thought, and I pressed into her mouth. She sucked on my finger, using her tongue as if it was my cock.

A groan erupted from my lips. "You're such a good girl," I said.

Her eyes shimmered at my words, and I loved seeing her like this.

I gave her a quick kiss that soon deepened with my need to taste myself on her tongue. When I pulled back, I put my cock away and told her I would be back before running to the bathroom and grabbing a wet cloth.

On my way back, I saw Kiaza coming quietly back up the stairs. She seemed startled when she saw me. "Hello, Grand Clarak," she said.

"Oh, hello," I said. "I thought you were headed to bed."

"I-I was," she stuttered. "I just decided to grab another drink before bed. Couldn't sleep."

I nodded. "Well, have a good night."

She quickly passed me and went to her room. That was odd, but I was too concerned with getting back to Sorcha to think too long about it.

When I returned, she was laid out across the bed, illuminated by the moonlight. She put her arm out for the cloth, but I pushed her away. "Let me."

She looked like she wanted to argue, but for once, she didn't. I wiped the cloth over her body, making sure she was totally clean before throwing it in the corner and laying down next to her.

"Are you okay?" I asked her.

She rolled to face me, a smile touching her lips. "Very."

"Good."

She rolled over and slipped into sleep quickly. I allowed myself to lay close, wrapping myself around her. I told myself this couldn't continue. This was a one-time thing, it had to be. We had a job to do, and feelings could complicate everything.

Though, as I fell asleep with my face buried in her hair, something told me that wouldn't be as easy as I hoped.

CHAPTER EIGHTEEN

SORCHA

MY EYES OPENED TO the early morning light filtering into the room. I blinked the sleep away, expecting to find a large body still next to me. When I rolled over, however, I was alone in a cold bed.

I sat up, stretching my arms above my head. Looking around, I found a bowl of oats, berries, and honey sitting on my nightstand. Though I still appreciated the gesture, without him here, it felt empty.

As I ate, my mind drifted back to the previous night. I felt like I couldn't wrap my head around it. I was so sure he hated me. We did flirt, but that was all part of the act, wasn't it?

But after we had such a good time last night, it was like a switch was flipped. It seemed like he was actually interested in me, not just in our charade. But then, I woke up alone this morning. I wasn't sure where that left us, but I planned on following his lead. Just because we hooked up doesn't mean anything changed.

When I finished eating, I got dressed to head out. Zarios and Damyr were already out front, preparing the horses.

"Good morning," Damyr said, noticing my arrival.

"Hello," I greeted.

I looked to Zarios, who met my eyes for a single second before looking away. *Okay.* I guess that was what we were going to do. Fine—I could pretend nothing happened just as easily as he could.

A few minutes later, Kiaza joined us as well as the rest of the guard and we headed out. The carriage ride was silent and tense, and I couldn't wait to get out.

We arrived to Mertis in the early evening. Mertis was much different than Sobury. It was a coastal town obviously important for imports and exports. The coast was lined with ships unloading fish and other goods. The cobblestone clicked loudly beneath the horses, the streets much busier here. Waves rolled up on the beach in the distance, the clear blue water foaming at the top. The salty sea smell was strong, and even in the middle of fall, it was warm and humid.

The carriage finally came to a halt, and we were let out.

"Welcome, Grand Clarak Zarios and his intended," a rust-colored minotaur in front of us called, though he strangely spoke as if it was a joke. He wore a loose white tunic and tanned white pants. The shirt was partially open, showing off his chest and the gold chains he wore underneath.

"Clarak Naram," Zarios greeted with more familiarity than I expected. "It's a pleasure, as always. This is my intended, Sorcha Yulean."

I fought my instinct to bow. "Lovely to meet you. Thank you for hosting us."

The pleasure is all mine," he said, bowing but taking my hand and kissing the back.

A low growl I felt in my bones made me jump and pull my hand away.

Naram only laughed, flipping his wavy long hair out of his face. "Oh, Zar, I'm just greeting our esteemed guest."

I whipped my head to Zarios, who looked like he was about to blow a horn.

"Zar?" I mouthed to him with wide eyes.

He gave me a scowl that told me to drop it, and I had to stop myself from laughing aloud.

"Come," Naram said, turning towards the large castle in front of us. "Let's get you settled."

We followed him through the large corridor. This building was decorated in hues of green and blue. Colored stone covered the floors, and seafoam green wallpaper lined the walls. There were gold chandeliers everywhere with crystals made to look like fish and water droplets. Unlike the other places I'd seen in Valcor, this place was made for show.

"Here are your rooms," Naram said as we approached a few cream-colored doors. "If you need anything, please find me personally." The eye contact he made with me as he said that made me squirm.

Zarios stepped in front of me, blocking my view. "Thank you, Naram. We will."

With another melodious laugh, he disappeared down the hall. Zarios let out an irritated huff and pushed open the door. This room was similar to the one in Sobury, with a small sitting area, a short table, a door leading to a bathroom, and the dreaded large bed. I gulped at the sight. I should have expected it, since it was implied we we're together, but it was such an inconvenience, especially after last night.

Zarios threw down our bags and flopped onto the couch hard. "Everything okay over there, Zar?" I asked with a smile as I sat beside him. I couldn't handle living in the same room with someone with this much tension, and I knew I needed to break it.

The less irritated huff he released told me it was working. "Don't start," he said. "I hate that nickname."

"Ah, but I think it's cute. Makes you seem less big and scary."

His narrow eyes cut to me. "But I *am* big and scary."

"I don't think so," I said honestly. "I think you're a stubborn ass most of the time, but I wouldn't call you scary."

He looked at me from behind those stupid bangs, hiding his expression. Though I couldn't see his eyes, being under that gaze made my lower belly warm.

I cleared my throat. "What's the plan?" I asked, trying to change the subject.

Zarios flopped back against the couch in exasperation. "This will be much more difficult. Mertis is known for their trade, so the paperwork on that is extensive. Looking at records may not be the right way to go."

I considered what he said. "If that's true, then maybe we need to take a different approach."

"Like what?"

I considered. "Walking around, I saw a lot more people around this castle," I said, thinking aloud.

"Yes. Mertis is the one territory with a large court. Because of their trade and their wealth, they care more about material things."

"Maybe that's our opening," I said. "People in court love to gossip. They love the idea of more power. Maybe they'll open up more if they think it will put them ahead."

He thinks for a moment. "That's actually a pretty good plan. We just need to be careful. We can't let anyone know our true intentions."

"Agreed, but I don't think it will be too difficult. As someone trying to gain an understanding of their new kingdom, who is also in line for the throne, I would be the perfect person to talk to."

Zarios smiled, and my heart skipped a beat. "That's genius."

I smiled back, unable to help it. Though I had the knowledge, I'd been ignored any time I tried to offer up any strategic moves. Having him acknowledge me and my ideas felt refreshing.

"We should start tonight," he continued, his mind working. "While we don't have any official plans, Naram loves a good time, and I'm sure something is going on."

"What do you mean?" I asked.

"Mertis is known for their large balls, but more importantly, their after-parties. If Naram is the same man I knew, I'm sure he has some kind of wild celebration planned."

I considered that. "That could be perfect. I'm sure those guest are the most aware about what he's up to."

"Exactly." It took me a moment to realize he was smiling at me and I was smiling back.

"When does it start?" I asked.

He cleared his throat and looked away. "A few hours."

"Perfect." I guess I was getting ready for a party.

Tonight, I decided on one of the skimpier dresses Lunar gave me, hoping to fit in further. This one was a deep royal blue with thin straps and a low neckline. The slits had gold chains this time, adorned with small pearls. I put a small amount of makeup on and left my hair down, deciding to skip the horns.

Zarios was in a pair of cream-colored pants that contrasted against his black fur, again bare chested. It seemed to be normal for men not to wear shirts here. Naram was the only one I'd seen who did, and he *barely* wore it.

His eyes perused my body as I approached, the way they always did, but they had a similar heat as last night. "That's a nice color on you," he said.

"Thank you," I said, sure I was blushing.

We headed out, walking in relative silence. We passed the real ballroom and headed to the other side of the of the palace.

"Where are we going?" I asked.

Zarios smirked. "You'll see."

He led me down a hall to a discreet-looking room, just like ours. I quirked my brow, but he paid me no mind as he pushed the door open. As he did, we were suddenly surrounded what looked to be another guest room.

"Why are we in another guest room?" I asked.

He sighed. "Would you please have a little faith?"

Though I was skeptical, I followed him to a bookshelf. He pulled down one of the books, and it opened like a latch. When he did, music filled the room, and I gasped in surprise. Inside was what looked to be a large pub, colored Magestone lanterns lining the edges, creating a vibrant atmosphere. There was a large bar in the center with a giant rack of alcohol behind it. People milled about, socializing and moving provocatively on the dance floor.

"Wow," I said, eyes wide. This looked more like Sage's scene than mine, but I'd been dragged through it enough to manage.

"I told you," he said. "Naram is always partying."

"I see." I looked around, trying to gauge where to start. "Any ideas?"

He hummed in thought. "I'm not sure. I must admit, court politics aren't my strength."

I snorted. "I could have guessed that."

He shoved my shoulder lightly. "Aren't we on the same team?"

"Yeah, sure." I continued assessing, but I knew I needed more. "Let's grab a drink."

He led me to the bar and ordered. I was handed a large glass of amber liquid. I shot half of it back in one go.

Zarios eyed me as he sipped on his own. "What?" I asked.

He shrugged. "You just drink very well."

"I train with a bunch of knights who drink daily, and it's better to keep up. I don't need to be perceived as any more different."

I shot the rest back. I wasn't sure why I said that last part. I was going to blame it on the alcohol, not how comfortable I felt with Zarios.

He eyed me for a moment then seemed to let it go. "Don't drink too much. We're here for work, not fun."

I scoffed. "I know that. I'm a good drinker."

I continued scanning the room as we talked. I spotted Naram sitting in the corner, surrounded by a core group. Though they might have better information, it was likely they were too loyal and comfortable in their position of power. No, I needed someone looking to get ahead.

My eyes landed on a minotaur with grey and white spotted fur. She was eyeing the table closely but made no move to join.

"I think I found my mark," I whispered to Zarios.

He nodded. "I'll try to keep Naram busy while you make the rounds. Just try not to draw too much attention. It's bad enough that you're human."

"It means everyone will want to talk to me," I said confidently, refusing to be shaken by his comment.

I ordered another drink before walking towards the table.

"Hello," I said as I approached.

"Oh, hi!" she said cheerily. "You're the Grand Clarak's intended right?"

"The one and only. May I?" I gestured to the seat next to her.

"Of course." I sat down and sipped my drink slowly. I didn't realize I'd had so much already and could feel it getting to me.

"I'm Sorcha," I said.

"Everyone knows that," she said with a smile. "I'm Irena."

"Nice to meet you. Have you been at court long?" I asked, trying to show an interest in her.

"Sort of," she sighed. Her tone was a bit slurred, telling me she was tipsy. "Almost a year, but between you and me, I might leave."

"Why?"

She took another long sip. "I came because my father, who owns Kings Fisher, wanted me and my sister to try to get closer to Naram, always hopeful to move his business forward."

"And it's not working?" I guessed.

"Well, it's working for one of us." She pointed to another female minotaur on the couch close to Naram. She had a similar gray coloring to her sister but kept her hair longer. "Fasmi got in day one."

"I see."

She groaned, hitting her head on the table. "I'm not even interested in Naram, much less in court politics, but because I room with her, I hear everything."

Interesting. "Moons, that must be annoying."

"It is." She slumped down over her drink. "But I won't bore you with the details."

I pulled my chair in a bit closer. "I'd love to know. Since I'm new to the kingdom, I'd like all the help I can get." I made my eyes wide and sincere.

She considered me for a moment, and I waited with bated breath, hoping she wouldn't think anything more of it.

"Really? To be honest, I'm terrible with secrets. I wanted to tell someone, but I didn't want to get my sister in trouble. But you won't tell, right?"

I grinned. "My lips are sealed."

"Great!" She caught the bartender walking by and ordered another drink for us both before slamming hers back. I almost felt bad for her, but I meant what I said, I wouldn't tell a soul unless it had to do with the case.

"So, apparently, Yama, who's Corin's best friend, slept with Corin's father!"

I spit my drink, choking on the mead inside. "What?" I couldn't help it—that was surprising.

"Exactly." She then launched into tales about who was hooking up with who, who was breaking up with who. While it was all interesting, it wasn't what I was looking for. Even still, I listened intently. Not only might she let something else slip, but I found I was genuinely interested in what she had to say.

"What about Naram?" I asked. In everything she'd said, she hadn't mentioned him once.

She looked a bit shy. "I wouldn't want to speak badly about the Clarak."

So there was something? I took my hand in hers. "I don't mean to put you in a bad spot, but I would love to know anything you could tell me. I'll be in this court soon, and I want to know exactly what I'm getting myself into."

She nodded. "I understand that. It can be hard if you don't know everything." She took a deep breath. "I don't hear much bad about Naram. Other than his bedroom pursuits, he seems to be loved by everyone, and he loves the Grand Clarak. They're best friends."

"They are?" I asked. That was new information. Why would Zarios suspect his best friend?

Before she could answer my question, a familiar face appeared behind Irena.

"Clarak Naram," I greeted quickly and loudly to signal he was here.

Irena quickly stopped and turned around. "Clarak Naram," she said with a respectful nod.

"Hello ladies. Having fun?" he asked.

He was now in an open black shirt and a tight pair of green pants. His long hair was still perfectly styled and wavy, falling around his large ivory horns. They curved further in than Zarios', but they seemed to fit him.

"Loads," Irena said. "This party is...great." It was obvious she was lying, even to me.

But Naram didn't say anything, he only let his gaze wander back to me. Unlike Zarios' gaze that made my lower belly heat, his did nothing for me, even though his interest was made clear.

"Irena," he said, finally looking at her. She seemed surprised he even knew her name, much less that he was talking to her. "Would you mind if I borrowed Sorcha for a moment?"

She looked to me, as if confirming I wanted her to go. I was touched by that. We hardly knew each other, but I think if I gave the word, she would say no, even to her Clarak. I offered her a small nod.

"Of course," she said. "I was thinking of heading out anyway."

She stood, brushing off her dress before waving and disappearing.

"Something I can help you with?" I asked.

He leaned against the table, right up in my space. "Just wanted to chat."

I scooted back in my chair as far as possible, but I was fairly trapped. "I don't see what you'd want to discuss with me."

"Many things. Like what you're doing with Zarios."

"Excuse me?" Could he see through our ruse?

"You're just really cute," he said, as if it was a fact. "And Zarios, well...he's a bit, shall we say, harsh. I'm just surprised."

I could feel indignation rise within me. "He's not harsh," I bit out. "Not always," I amended.

Naram's laugh was loud and full. "You sure are feisty for a human."

"And you are sure bold, hitting on the Grand Clarak's intended."

He shrugged. "I like to take chances." Suddenly, he was much closer, his snout inches from my face. Even though he was very handsome, he again didn't give me the same feeling I got from...

"*What are you doing?*" a sharp, grumbling voice said from behind me.

CHAPTER NINETEEN

ZARIOS

I WATCH SORCHA SAUNTER off towards the gray-haired woman. She was wearing another dress from Valcor, and it looked much different on her than it did on minotaur women.

Her thighs didn't stick out of the slits as far, so I only caught a glimpse every once in a while, which felt somehow more scandalous. The top also sat lower on her slimmer frame, and her breasts were larger compared to the rest of her body, making the plunging neckline much sultrier.

I thought it would be best not to follow her, since people would be less likely to talk if I was around. I scanned the hazy, smoke-filled room. This hadn't been my scene in a long time. I thought back to the days it was.

Naram, Damyr, and I used to be very close. We'd come to Mertis often for nights like these. We would train during the day and indulge at night. Though it seemed Naram still preferred this lifestyle, I gave it up long ago. It almost destroyed Damyr and made me realize I should quit too.

Speaking of Damyr, he was over with Naram now, in a booth surrounded by others. When I met his gaze, he waved me over, and everyone turned.

I let out an exhaustive huff. *Great*. I wandered over.

"Grand Clarak Zar," Naram said in a mocking tone. "Thank you for blessing us with your presence."

Damyr broke into a loud laugh, and I huffed my amusement. "Very funny." I sat next to them and was passed a drink quickly.

"So how are things?" Naram asked. "I heard you're having issues with a group of thieves."

I grunted, taking a deep sip. "I would prefer not to discuss work." Normally, I wouldn't mind, but with so much at stake, I couldn't reveal what was really going on. The genuine way he asked, however, made me feel more confident that he wasn't involved. Knowing him for so long gave me the ability to tell when he was lying, and it seemed he wasn't.

"Fair enough," he said, raising his glass before taking a sip. He didn't press further, which made me internally sigh with relief. It didn't seem like he was prying for information for any particular reason. We weren't out of the woods yet, but it gave me hope.

Everyone went back to their conversations, and my eyes drifted to Sorcha, who was laughing loudly. Her smile made her look so carefree.

"She's very pretty. You're lucky," Naram commented over his glass.

"She is and I am," I said, trying to keep my jealousy at bay. This was all pretend, after all, and I wasn't the jealous type anyway.

"Zarios," I heard called from behind me.

I turned to see Naram's brother. "Kian," I greeted.

He jumped into small talk. He'd always been chatty, and this was no different. Damyr chimed in every once and a while, but he stayed relatively quiet.

I realized after a while that Naram had walked away. I didn't think much of it until I turned my eyes back to Sorcha. The minotaur woman was gone, and Naram took her place.

Even from here, I could tell he was turning on the charm. He'd always been good with what he called 'conquests'. Men, women, didn't matter—when he set his eyes on a target, I'd never seen him miss. He'd never been one for stealing someone who was already spoken for, but it seemed he'd had a change of heart since we last met.

I watched as he pushed his hair from his eyes and said something with a wink. My body boiled. I tried to be rational. While, to the world, we were intended, she wasn't *really* mine—even though every instinct inside told me that was a lie. When she smiled back at him, I couldn't ignore it any longer.

I excused myself from Kian and marched straight to the table.

"I like taking chances," I heard him say. He leaned in closer than I liked before I reached them in this crowded space.

"What are you doing?" I asked, my voice low and rumbling.

Sorcha jumped back, her deep brown eyes wide.

Naram made no such move, his eyes cutting casually to me. "We're just chatting," he said with a smile.

My eyes narrowed. I didn't understand. I knew we didn't talk as much, and as a Clarak, he wasn't one to take risks, putting us on opposite sides of the table at times, but he'd never been the type to do something like this.

Sorcha's eyes were firmly on her drink. "If you'll excuse us, Naram," I said, "I'd like to have a word with my intended."

He raised his brows and didn't make any effort to move. "I hope I haven't upset you," he said. "I just wanted to have a little chat. Your intended is just so...intriguing."

Fuck it.

I didn't know what his problem was, but I didn't like it. I knew I wasn't being rational. I knew I would upset Sorcha, but something in my brain wasn't working right when I decided to pick Sorcha up like I did on that first day and move to leave. Whatever I'd told myself yesterday about keeping my distance had been thrown out the window.

As I lifted her, she gasped then started yelling and flailing. "Put me down!" she yelled over the loud music. "Zarios!"

I didn't listen. Even angry, my name from her lips soothed me. I held her as we exited the dark, loud space into the empty quiet hall. I continued walking, heading back to our rooms. She quieted when we entered the foyer, probably more aware of our surroundings, but I had no such thoughts. I wanted nothing but to get her alone.

After what felt like the longest walk of my life, we were in front of our door. Once I shut it behind me, I set her down. Her round cheeks were flushed, her eyes narrowed. She was pissed, and I couldn't help but find that cute.

"What was that?" she asked, all but yelling her displeasure. "You can't just carry me off like that. I didn't even do anything. He came to talk to me! I was focused on the mission, unlike you, who—"

Her words halted as I leaned in, pressing her to the wall. She looked as if she wanted to say something but was lost for words. My gaze dropped to her full lips, replaying last night in my head.

I pressed my hand to the wall next to her head and used the other to tilt her chin up. I leaned in and brought my lips to hers. She stayed frozen at first. I almost pulled away, thinking I'd made a mistake, but after a moment, her lips met mine.

She tasted of mead and something spicy that was all her own. I deepened the kiss with my tongue, needing to taste more of her. She melted beneath me, making me want her even more.

Her hands snaked up my shoulders, and I reached for her thighs, lifting her up and pinning her to the wall behind us. Her legs came around me, but they couldn't reach to hook together.

My touch moved up until I could feel the swell of her ass, fingers digging into the meaty flesh. I could feel my cock rub against her cunt, only a few thin strips of cotton separating us.

I kissed her once more before lowering, mouthing over her jaw back to bite her ear. I chomped down a bit hard, testing her. She released a sharp gasp and pressed her body into mine, trying to find her own friction.

Interesting.

I worked down further, kissing down her neck over her shoulder as she shuddered beneath me. I pulled away and shifted to hold her with one hand. We sat there for a moment, the only sound between us our labored breathing as I just...stared, from her deep, obsidian hair that had gotten a slight bit longer since we started this journey to her slightly round cheeks and pointed chin. Her eyes were dark but alive in a way I couldn't explain. I could get lost in their depths and would happily meet my end there.

My hand moved up and traced the small strap of her dress. It followed all the way down to the swell of her breasts. Unable to help myself, I lowered the garment until her breasts popped free. She gasped as I did, but I couldn't tear my gaze away. They were round and fell a bit to the sides, with dusky pink points for nipples.

When I ran my thumb over one of them, she let out the smallest moan, one I desperately craved more of. I brought my tongue down and lapped over it as she leaned into my touch, rewarding me with her moans.

I continued to lick at her nipple and gripped the other, plucking it with my fingers.

"Zarios," she moaned. She gripped my fur hard, pulling enough to sting, but I relished the feeling. I switched, tonguing her other nipple. When I looked up, she had her eyes down on me, twinkling in the moonlight. I bit down hard again, and I watched as her flush deepened and her mouth opened on a sharp inhale.

I needed more. Dropping to my knees, I hiked her legs up to my shoulders. She grabbed onto my horns for support, and the touch made my cock weep. I used one of my hands to move the slit of her skirt over and tossed it to the side. She wore a thin, pink pair of panties, and I could see a touch of dampness from her arousal. I leaned in and dragged my long, flat tongue across the fabric.

Her taste was sweet like honey and a bit musky. It drove me mad. I ran my tongue over the fabric a few more times, teasing around the top before moving lower.

"Moons," she cursed. "Please."

"Please what?" I asked.

She didn't answer, so I continued.

When she finally couldn't stand it anymore, she stuttered out, "P-please. I want to feel you."

I growled, low and deep. "Of course, Princess."

I pulled her underwear down, revealing her to me. Her cunt was as mesmerizing as I remembered, glistening with her juices. I licked up the middle, and without the fabric to dull her taste, my head spun. This was something I could become addicted to *quickly*.

I continued my exploration, tasting her freely, stealing her beautiful moans. I remembered how she felt about having her clit played with and dove for it, wanting her to be a writhing mess beneath me.

Soon, I worked down to her opening, shoving my tongue inside her. She was so tight and hot. Imagining my cock inside her almost made me come then and there.

"Just like that," she ground out. I continued fucking her as her walls squeezed my tongue, throwing her towards the edge.

Her fingers snaked down to touch her clit, but my hand flew up and caught it. I didn't need any help to wring her of pleasure.

I brought my tongue back and started working it again. I nipped her here lightly, and she screamed.

"Do you like pain with your pleasure, Princess?" I asked.

She didn't answer, so I brought my hand down sharply on her ass. The cracking sound rang through the space, and her resulting cry was tinged with pleasure. "I asked if you liked it. Don't make me repeat myself."

"Or what?"

My laugh was dark. "Would you like to find out?"

CHAPTER TWENTY

SORCHA

ZARIOS HELD ME UP against the wall, my legs draped across his shoulders. I was so close to falling off the edge.

This felt like a shock after ignoring what happened last night. We would need to talk about it, but I couldn't think about that right now. I couldn't think about anything else. I knew he'd asked me a question, but I barely heard him. I could only focus on my pleasure. He still had one of my hands pinned to the wall, and something about it pleased me.

"I guess so," he said, bringing my focus back to him. His hair still covered his eyes, hiding his full expression, but I could see the intensity behind them. I'd never been looked at like this. I couldn't even pinpoint what was in his gaze. Lust, adoration, worship? I wasn't sure, but it made me melt.

"If you want me to stop, you tell me to stop, understand?"

I nodded.

"No, Princess," he said. "I need the words."

"I'll tell you to stop."

He hummed, pleased. I had no idea what he was planning, but whatever it was, I craved it.

Suddenly, his palm came back down on the side of my ass. I let out a shrill moan. The area where his hand landed stung and felt a bit warm. Though it was painful, there was a pleasurable edge to it that had me soaked.

He did it a few more times, always landing in the same spot. Finally, he brought that same hand up between my legs. I could hear the wetness as his fingers danced over my clit then down to my opening. None of it was enough to get me close. When I tried to move for more friction, his other hand moved up to hold down my middle.

I looked down in time to watch him pull his fingers from me and lick them clean. My head spun with the image. "That tells me you like it," he said. "But I want to hear it from your lips. Do you like the pain?"

Did I? I'd only had sex once, with Dorlin, another recruit in my year. He was the first one who didn't treat me differently, and while it was fun, there were no real sparks between us, and he ended up being sent to a city out west. Outside of that, I had no real experience to speak of.

But now, here... "Yes." I said. "Well, I think. It's sort of new."

His eyes flashed when I said that. "Good girl, Princess," he murmured. "I knew you could be honest."

The butterflies in my stomach were in full effect. The mixture of the name he used to tease me and the praise that came across as genuine turned me on in a way I couldn't describe.

He leaned back in and began feasting on me once more. That was the only word I could use to describe it. His tongue lashed over my clit hard. It was much bigger than a human tongue, with a bit of a harder texture.

He bit down on me once more before moving down, fucking me with his tongue in earnest. I was so close to falling off the edge, but I'd never been able to get off like this. I was about to reach for my clit once more when Zarios' hand crept up and circled it with his fingers.

It only took a few more movements for me to fall apart, but my orgasm hit me hard, racking through my body. It was like all my nerve endings sparked and filled me with light. I felt liquid gush from me as my vision darkened at the edges. It was like the whole world vanished and it was only us.

When I came down, I slumped back against the wall, held up only by Zarios.

He pulled away and lifted me easily, carrying me to the bed. He set me down, and I sank into it, turning onto my stomach. I closed my eyes, feeling wrung out in the best way.

Zarios crawled up the bottom of the bed, and I assumed he was joining me to sleep. Instead, my eyes flew open when he gripped my hips and pulled them up until I was on my hands and knees.

"What are you doing?" I asked.

He didn't answer, spreading my legs and lowering himself to his back behind me. I hovered over his snout until I felt him lick up my pussy to my clit. "I know you can give me one more," he groaned.

He pushed my thighs further apart and continued licking me as I moaned loudly. I was so raw from my first orgasm, it felt like too much, too soon. It was almost painful, but in a way, I found it exciting and erotic.

This time, he kept his focus on my clit. He circled it with lots of pressure. Until last night, I didn't know I could feel this good, and now, I feared I would never get enough.

I moaned as one of his large fingers entered me. I was so wet, he slid right in, but I still stretched around him. His digits were so impossibly large, it made me worry what his cock might feel like.

He soon added another finger, pumping into me with abandon. The stimulation was too much and not enough at the same time.

"Zarios!" I cried. "It's so good."

He growled, and the vibrations only added to it all. He bent his fingers slightly and grazed my G-spot. My back rolled off the bed. He seemed to notice and continued what he was doing, hitting that spot with each stroke.

It was too much. I broke. I broke into a million pieces, barely held together by the man inside me. Wetness pooled from me, and Zarios licked it all up, going past my first orgasm, sending me barreling into another. Neither were as strong as the first, but they completely drained me.

Suddenly, he sat up and pinned my hands above my head, forcing me down so my front was pressed to the bed, my ass in the air. He moved so quickly, I could barely process. I heard his buckle unlatch and his zipper hiss as he pulled it down.

I turned to watch his large cock fall out, and my eyes widened. It was even larger than I remembered. It had a blunt tip, a ridge wrapped around the middle. There were two silver bars with small balls on each side sticking out. My cunt clenched thinking about how it would feel inside me.

I swallowed. He got closer, and I felt him rub himself against my ass. His hand wrapped around his cock as he milked himself above me. After only a few strokes, he came all over my back. He came much more than a human, and I could feel as it pooled on me and dripped from my body.

He growled. "What are you doing to me, Princess?"

I could ask you the same, I thought. I'd meant to say it aloud, but exhaustion took over and carried me to sleep before I could.

CHAPTER TWENTY-ONE

ZARIOS

I AWOKE WRAPPED AROUND Sorcha. Even my tail circled her ankle. I pulled away, careful not to wake her. When I got up, I took a moment to look down at her. She was gorgeous.

But that was still a distraction.

I left and went to the shower. I couldn't stop thinking about the previous night. Her taste, her smell, her sounds. It played on a loop since it happened. I even dreamed about it—except my dream ended with me buried in that sweet cunt.

I shook my head as I lathered soap over my fur. This was a distraction. She was my intended in name only. When we caught the person attacking the kingdom, she would probably end up with some human lord.

The thought made me seethe, so much that I crushed the bar of soap to pieces in my grip. This was a problem. I couldn't become attached. Attachments meant mistakes, and I couldn't afford any of those. Last night should have proven that to me. I couldn't react like that any time another man talked to her. It wasn't rational.

I finished my shower quickly, dressed, and moved to the bedroom.

When I got there, Sorcha was sitting against the headboard, her hair mussed like it was last night. Her night slip hung low in front of her, showing a bit of her breast.

"Morning," I said.

"Good morning."

We stared at each other in silence. What was there to say? I shifted on my feet as she played with her nails.

"About the last few nights," she started. "It was..." She trailed off.

"A way to get it out of our system," I said, finishing her thought.

Her eyes widened for a moment before settling to neutral. "Yes. That's all. We've just been...close."

"Yes," I agreed, my tongue feeling heavy with the lie. "It's better for us not to repeat it."

"Agreed." Something flickered in her eyes briefly, something that might have mirrored this sadness I was feeling. "We can go back to normal."

I cleared my throat. "Agreed."

The silence was tense. Everything I said felt wrong, but I knew it was right. "I have a meeting in the morning, but we have the main event in the afternoon in town. I'll be back around eleven, and we can do some walking around beforehand."

"Sounds good." She hopped off the bed and went to the bathroom, clicking it closed and effectively shutting me out.

I quickly grabbed my things and left. As I did, my stomach dropped. I stood there for a moment behind the closed door, allowing myself to wallow in my feelings for a few seconds more. That conversation felt wrong, and walking away from it felt even worse, but I couldn't allow myself to make a mistake, to get caught up in anything that felt as real and raw as she did.

I had lied about the meeting, just needing to put some space between us before I did something unintelligent.

Like toss her back on the pillows and plow her through the bed.

When I finally got myself moving, I decided to look for Naram and found him exactly where I suspected he'd be—lounging out on the patio, drink in hand, bathing in the sun.

"Zar," he said, waving his drink in greeting. "I didn't think I'd see you until the afternoon, not with the way you hauled your intended from the party last night."

Naram shrugged. "I wouldn't have done what I did if someone didn't need it."

My brow rose. "I'm sorry?"

He set his drink down, sitting up a bit. "It was obvious you needed a little...push."

"A push?" I parroted.

"Yes," he said, sounding exasperated. "We've been friends for a long time. I could tell something was off, so I tested her."

"Why?" I asked. I didn't like the idea of anyone testing Sorcha.

"I worried she was just with you for the title. You're not much of a catch," he said with a wink.

"She's royalty in Peradona," I said flatly.

"Second in line," he countered.

"She doesn't care about that." I was sure of it.

"Oh, I could tell," he said with a laugh.

My brows drew up in confusion. "How?"

"Because someone only in it for the power would have easily folded to my charm," he said simply.

I let out a short huff. "Not everyone falls for that."

He quirked his brow. "Have you ever seen it not work?"

I stayed silent because I couldn't argue. "I wanted to see if she was actually interested in you, or your title. And she passed."

I crossed my arms over my chest. "How could you tell? Just because she didn't fall for your flirting doesn't mean anything." I didn't know why I was arguing with him. It was better for him to think it was real, but for some reason, I felt the need to know what he saw, to know why he thought that.

"The whole time we talked, her eyes rarely strayed from you."

His words made me pause. I hadn't noticed. My mind replayed every moment we'd been together. Not the times we'd been together in front of others, but the moments when no one was looking. The unnecessary hand holding, the lighthearted jabs we took at each other. I hadn't put much thought into it, but maybe that did all mean something.

"So that still leaves me wondering," Naram said, interrupting my thoughts, "as to why you're here instead of there with that beautiful woman."

I sat down in the lounge chair next to him with a sigh. I obviously couldn't reveal our plans, but it would be nice to have someone to speak with.

"We had a bit of an argument," I confessed.

"Oh, tell me everything," he insisted.

I sighed. "It wasn't even really a fight. It was just...tense. I needed some space."

He nodded. "Did you try to talk about it?"

I cocked my head at him. "Talk?"

He let out his own sigh, setting his drink down. "My poor, non-communicative Grand Clarak. Sometimes, and by sometimes, I mean all the time, you don't communicate the things you're feeling."

Communicate my feelings? "But what if they aren't logical?"

He shrugged. "The best ones usually aren't."

I thought about his words. He was right, but I didn't know what I would say, what I could say. A servant came around and brought tea and breakfast. We ate, Naram adding some gin to his tea before drinking it.

I scrunched my face. "I can't believe you're still able to drink like that."

He laughs. "The trick is to never stop. Pickles the liver and keeps you young forever."

We shared a laugh. He swirled his glass. "Damyr seems better now," he commented.

I sighed. "He is, I think. Did he stay after we left?"

"No, actually," Naram said. "He left not long after, I assume right back to his room. I'm glad he seemed okay.

After everything, I worried he would go right back to his old ways. Or hate us."

I shook my head. "Why would he? We did what was best for him."

"People don't always sees it that way. But he seemed better," he conceded.

I nodded, thinking back to all those years ago. I had just become Grand Clarak and quit the partying life all together. Naram and Damyr were still very much in it, staying in Mertis. That was, until Damyr's father, Chamil, the previous Clarak of Mertis, reached out to me. Apparently, Damyr wasn't just indulging on his days off. He was ignoring his responsibilities, going on multi-day benders, from drinking, to drugs, to brothels. It was getting out of hand, and that was when Chamil asked Naram and I to do something for him.

After much discussion and many failed attempts at keeping him away from it all, his father helped us send him up north to Thvetharion. It was emptier out there, and he would have some time to clear his mind and focus on what was important.

Chamil left his post not long after, and Naram became Clarak of Mertis. It was my first choosing ceremony, and while we were friends, he was objectively the most qualified. He also won in the arena, which could hardly be challenged. Though he seemed like your average charming guy, he was a beast beneath it all.

When Damyr came back, I offered him a job as head of guard in the castle. He took it, and he has seemed alright ever since. I was proud of him for getting away from that lifestyle.

"Well," he said, snapping me out of my musings, "I'm just glad it seems to be water under the bridge."

"I agree."

We finished breakfast, and I excused myself to find Sorcha once more. With some time away, I felt as if my lust filled brain has had a break. What I did this morning was the right thing. I was sure of it.

At least, I was until I walked back into our rooms. She wore a yellow dress today. This one was from Peradona, with a fuller skirt and a slightly higher neckline. The sleeves were slightly puffed. She looked like she did when we met, which now seemed so unlike her.

"You ready?" she asked, pulling her slightly heeled shoes on.

"Yes," I said. "Is that what you're wearing?"

She paused to look at me. "Is there something wrong with this?"

"No," I quickly amended. "I just want you to be comfortable."

"Well, I'm plenty comfortable," she said, lifting the skirt in a practiced way and stepping around me towards the door. There was obviously something wrong, but I wasn't sure what or how to even ask.

I followed her out, and she walked at a much brisker speed than normal. I easily kept up, but normally, I was slowing my pace for her.

Once we left the main entrance, she didn't know where to go, so she paused, letting me take the lead. The silence between us felt tense, and I hated it. The only sound was the shifting of her skirts. "What did you have planned?" she asked. She never made eye contact with me.

I didn't have a plan, but now, I felt like I needed to do something. "Would you like to go to the pier?" I said quickly.

"Lead the way," she gestured. No attitude, no fight back. None of her normal spark.

I huffed in annoyance but led us there anyway. With the celebration of the Grand Clarak's intended happening that night, it was much less busy than normal. The beach was almost empty, save for a few lone fishers.

The water glittered, clear and blue. The sand was soft beneath my hooves. Even holding it up, I could see her skirt dragging through the sand, and the heeled shoes made it hard to walk.

"Would you like to wade?" I asked.

She looked to the bottom of her skirt. "I'm fine."

I shrugged and bent down to roll my pants up a bit. While bent, I noticed her staring at my ass. It warmed something in me, but that feeling needed to be stamped out. I walked into the water. Though the air was a bit cool, the water was still warm from the summer.

She stood on the edge, right where the water couldn't touch. "The water's nice," I taunted.

"Great," she said, crossing her arms.

We both watched as a large wave rolled in, and before she could react, it rolled up higher and swept the bottom of her skirt and on her feet. She sighed loudly.

"I guess you might as well come in now," I commented, trying to keep my laugh to myself.

She grumbled something I didn't pick up as she plopped down in the sand and pulled her shoes and socks off.

I walked over and reached my hand out to help her up. She glanced at it for a moment before helping herself up and stepping around me towards the water.

This woman. At least she seemed a bit more like herself. I was sort of glad she didn't take my hand.

I followed her in as she waded to mid-calf, her dress floating around her.

"The water is nice," she said after a moment.

"I told you," I said. "You don't have to be so stubborn all the time."

She sniffed. "I'm not *always* stubborn."

The laugh that came out was involuntary. She looked at me, mouth open. "What?"

I looked at her in confusion. "You are the most stubborn woman I've ever met."

She gasped. "Am not."

"Are too."

She narrowed her eyes. "How mature."

"It's not always bad," I said. "It makes you strong too."

She didn't say anything to that, just letting her gaze go back to the waterline.

Soon, another large wave rolled in and pulled her skirt. She lost her footing. I went to catch her and lost mine as well. She screamed as I twisted us and fell into the water on my back, her on top.

We sank, but I quickly scrambled us back up. The water wasn't deep, so when we sat up we were easily seated above the water.

Sorcha brushed her hair out of her face and turned to me. My fringe was blocking the view a bit, so I moved it out of the way.

We stared at each other for a moment before we both broke out into uncontrollable laughter. We must have looked mad, in the ocean, off season, in regular clothing, but it was hilarious.

"We may need to change," I commented as I stopped.

"We may," she agreed.

"Why don't we pick something up so we don't have to go all the way back to the castle?"

"If you're sure," she said.

"Of course. You in?"

She stood and held her hand out to me this time. "Let's go."

I took it. "Let's."

CHAPTER TWENTY-TWO
SORCHA

WE MADE OUR WAY from the beach to the main pier. It was ginormous, made of a dark wood that stood above the ocean. There were a lot of different shops and food stalls around. I couldn't help but stop and look at each one. Maybe once we had some clothes, we could peruse a few.

Zarios pulled me into a store called A-pier-al Boutique, a small shop lined with different garments, hats, and jewelry.

"Hello," the shopkeeper said as we walked in. They were much shorter and older than Zarios, with wrinkles along their eyes and dark brown fur. "How can I help you, Grand Clarak?"

"Hello, Tufan," Zarios greeted. "My intended and I took a bit of a fall in the ocean, and we were looking for a change of clothes."

"Oh my," they said, taking us in. "It seems. I'm certain I can find something. Your intended would probably fit into something made for calves."

My eyes widened at Zarios, but Tufan paid us no mind, shuffling through the store to collect some options. They came back with a bunch of garments. "One of these should work," they said. "If not, I can pull some others."

We were led to a changing room in the back with only one, large door. "I apologize, I only have one room since we're so small, but I figured you could share."

My cheeks pinkened, but Zarios said, "No problems. We'll come find you if we need you."

Zarios took the pile of clothes and led us into the room. For a dressing room, it was large, with a bench off to the side and a rack to hang things, but it felt like we were right on top of each other. The entire back wall was a mirror.

Looking at us, we looked a mess. My hair was wet and stringy, and my dress was silk, so the water made it splotchy as it dried unevenly. Zarios wasn't much better. On our walk, his hair had begun to dry, and it now stuck up in weird spots.

Zarios hung everything then turned to face me. "What would you like to do?" he asked.

"I'm sorry?"

"I can change first while you turn, or you can go first."

I hadn't thought of that. I warred with myself. Though I thought it could be a slippery slope to change together like this, but I didn't want to come across as a prude. "Just turn around," I said finally.

His tail flicked behind him, but he nodded. "Very well."

He passed me the first dress then stood in the corner, facing away from the mirror. The dress was black and a lot like the ones I'd already worn. This one had a high neckline with no sleeves and a sash that went around the back.

I grabbed for the ties in the dress I had on but could barely reach. I'd asked the woman who came in this morning to help me dress, though I had to explain it to her. Another reason I despised these garments. At least the ones here were easy to remove and put on yourself.

I continued my attempts at freeing myself to no success. I sighed and threw my hands into the skirts. Was it childish? Probably, but that didn't make it any less frustrating.

"Need help, Princess?" I heard him ask.

He must have heard my shuffling. "I'm fine," I said more confidently than I felt.

When I finally managed to grab hold of one of the ties, I dropped it when I went for the other. This went on for longer than I'd like to admit.

"We're going to be here all day if you don't let me help you," he said, rocking back and forth on his hooves.

I groaned. "Fine. I can't reach the ties."

He faced me and I put my back to him.

I felt his large hands on my back as he started pulling at the strings. I remembered how they felt on me yesterday. On my thighs, between my legs.

He fidgeted for a few moments, but nothing loosened. "Moons," he cursed. "How do you get yourself in this blasted thing?"

I laughed. "You need to undo the knot at the bottom and unlace the whole thing starting from the left. And for the record, *I* didn't. I had help."

He froze when I said that. I could see his angry expression in the mirror. "Who helped you?" he grumbled.

The sound strangely went right down to my cunt. "The maid who came in this morning," I told him.

He nodded and swallowed. Soon after, the ties were loosened, and I had to hold the front to keep it up.

I gazed up at him, and my breath caught when I met his gaze. He had that look in his eye I'd seen more often in the past few nights. Though I wanted to lean back against him and drop the front of my dress right then, I didn't. I couldn't.

Two nights ago, I thought things between us were changing. There seemed to be something there that wasn't there before. But the next morning, he brushed it off as if it never happened.

And then, last night, I was carried off in a room full of people. I let myself get carried away...and let him change his mind in the morning. Though the logical part of me agreed there was nothing good that would come of having feelings for each other, the other part of me craved him in a way I couldn't reason with. I couldn't allow that part of me to get hurt again.

"You can turn back around," I said briskly.

A hand ran up my shoulder from the middle of my arm, making me shiver without meaning to. His gaze stayed on me, and he made no effort to move. "What if I didn't want to?" he asked slowly.

I let out a heavy sigh before I turned around. He took a step back, giving me a bit of room. "I had fun last night," I started, "and the night before. But I don't think I can do it again. I can't..." I didn't even know what to say. I couldn't separate myself from my feelings? I couldn't imagine how painful it would be to lose you after all of this?

Hurt flashed in his eyes. "You can't what?" he asked.

I couldn't say anything. I didn't know what I would say. "A secret for a secret?" he asked.

I nodded, moving my eyes down to my knotted hands. A secret for a secret.

"I thought I could quit you after one time," he said. It hurt, until, "but I was wrong."

My gaze met his. He seemed genuine. I swallowed hard. "I can't keep doing this if you keep pulling away from me the next morning."

His face remained the same. I wished I could tell what he was thinking, but he gave nothing away. It was as if time had stopped between us. I was holding my breath, waiting for him to respond.

"What if I stopped pulling away?" he asked.

I blinked. "You would stop?" I asked.

He nodded. "I don't want to pull away anymore either, and I'm sorry I did. I didn't mean to hurt you."

His hand ran up my cheek, and I leaned into his touch. "Promise?" I asked, gazing up at him.

He didn't answer. He pulled me into a hard kiss. This one felt different than others. Before, it always felt like there was some tension between us. Now that it was gone, though, the kiss felt more raw, more real. His tongue found its way in my mouth, and I melted into him.

I dropped my arms, and my dress fell to the floor with a wet plop. My stays went with it, so I was left only in my underwear.

I could hear the clinking of a belt and the hiss of a zipper. When I pulled away, Zarios was left fully bare. My eyes worked down from his large chest, over his strong middle, all the way down to his long cock.

My face felt like it would catch fire. I quickly glanced away.

I bit my bottom lip. He gripped my chin and pulled it free, stepping closer. "Don't hurt yourself," he said.

"I thought you liked when I hurt?" I challenged.

He huffed, not quite annoyed, but not quite amused. "I don't like seeing you hurt, but I do like causing you a bit of pain. And I think you like it too."

Even though I knew this could still end badly, I let him pull me in. "You are something else, Princess."

"You know I hate when you call me that," I gasped, though something about it in this context felt different.

His fingers trailed down my middle between my thighs. They slid to my center, under my underwear, and right through my wetness. I gasped, gripping his shoulders tighter.

"This tells me something different," he said. His fingers rounded my clit, and I melted into him.

I whimpered as he pulled them out. He looked to his fingers and made eye contact with me as he brought them to his lips, licking me off.

It was somehow one of the hottest things I'd ever seen. My gaze drifted back down to his cock, so thick and full. I couldn't help but wonder...

"Do you want to taste me?" he asked.

I nodded, having no idea how he read my mind like that.

"On your knees."

I sank down, my dress pillowing my knees, so I remained comfortable. He gripped his length and held it in front of me as his other hand snaked under my jaw, his thumb pressing into my mouth. "Open."

I opened for him, rolling my tongue out slightly. He guided his length to my lips and I let my tongue roll over the tip. A drop of pre-cum landed on my tongue, the musky flavor filling my senses.

Though I wanted to do this, my nerves began getting the better of me. I'd never done this. My only previous experience consisted of fumbling hands and didn't last very long. He hissed as we made contact, which made me feel more confident.

I took more of him, his cock stretching my mouth wide. When I reached the first bar, I ran my tongue over it, making him shiver. The metal was cool compared to the rest of him. I pulled back and looked up at him. At this angle, I could see more of his face than normal. His brow bone was prominent, and his eyes were slightly large.

When I went back down, I took him further, feeling him press against the back of my throat. I went a bit further, making it almost to his ridge.

His hand gripped my hair, easing me on and off his cock. The control he had over me wasn't something I expected to enjoy, but surprisingly, I found I did. He pulled me all the way off, a strand of saliva still connecting us.

"If you want me to stop, hit my thigh," he said. "Understand?"

"Yes," I said, my voice hoarse.

"Good little Princess." His hand came up and gripped my hair before he plunged me down on his shaft, going down so far that he hit the back of my throat. I gagged around him, but he only pulled me back a slight bit before pulling me down even further.

He continued like that, fucking my face with abandon. It made me feel used in the hottest way.

"I'm going to come," he said in warning.

He pulled me back, but I pressed down, wanting to taste him. He seemed to catch the hint and picked up his pace. He pumped thrice more before he pushed almost down my throat and let out a harsh groan. He came down my throat, and I swallowed as much as I could. As I did, my throat squeezed his length harder, making him call out louder. Eventually, it was too much, and it spilled from the corners of my mouth.

He pulled out and jerked himself once, spilling the last bit of cum on my face. I wiped it with my finger and put it in my mouth, never breaking eye contact.

"Moons, Princess," he said. "What do you do to me?" He barreled towards me, lifting me and setting me on the bench in the changing room. He pulled the black fabric belt from one of my skirt options and tied my hands with it in a neat little bow.

"Hands above your head," he instructed, and I easily followed. I felt so laid out and exposed as he spread my thighs. He tore my underwear clean off, dropping the shreds to the floor. Then, his tongue was on me.

I had to turn my mouth to the side, covering it with my shoulder. He ate me as if I was his last meal. The cold I'd felt from being wet melted away, leaving me hot from the inside out.

His tongue fucked in and out of me. It was so long and thick, it stretched me slightly. "Please," I whispered, trying to stay quiet. Though we were in the back of the store, I didn't want to draw attention.

"Do you need something, Princess?" he asked. "I've never known you not to say exactly what you want."

Moons, this mouthy minotaur. "I need to come. Please," I begged. As much as I wished to fight him, he was right. I knew what I needed.

He growled low and fucked me harder with his tongue. One of his hands moved up to my clit, circling it the way he did the night before.

That was all it took. My orgasm rolled through me like a tidal wave, sending pleasure through all my nerves. He didn't stop, continuing even when it was too much. I tried pushing away, but he held tight, rolling me from one orgasm into the next.

It was so intense—almost too intense. He finally pulled back, licking his lips as he did. I slumped back against the bench, feeling utterly boneless.

A few seconds later, a knock came at the door. My eyes widened. "Everything okay in there?" Tufan called.

I looked to Zarios, who only smirked. "Amazing," he said in a suggestive tone. "We'll be out soon."

"Very well." I could hear his hoofbeats as they walked away.

"That was close," I breathed, standing to dress in earnest this time.

Zarios stepped into his pants. "I'm sure they knew."

I paused, my eyes wide. "What?"

He shrugged. "It's common for intended mates to be unable to keep their hands off each other. That's also why no one questioned our disappearance in Sobury. They expected us to disappear like that."

"You don't think they were...listening, do you?" Though, in honesty, the thought sort of excited me.

"I wouldn't guess. But who knows?"

Once we were finished dressing, we headed out.

Tufan was there with a smile on their face. "Did you find what you were looking for?" they asked.

"Yes," Zarios said. "Thank you." He threw a few gold pieces on the table, and we left.

We exited the shop and walked down the cobblestone path. I was happy to be out of those clothes. I wasn't even sure why I put that dress on. I was so angry, I couldn't think about being there. I didn't want anything to remind me of him, so I slid on one of my old dresses. Though I didn't like wearing them normally, in the moment, it made me feel separated from him in the way I needed.

Now, in more comfortable attire, my nose led me to something sweet and fried. I found the source at a stall with a large fish as the sign. "The Sweetfish," it read.

I moved towards the building, Zarios following close behind. I could see small fried balls on a stick sprinkled with sugar.

We ordered two and continued our walk. When I bit into it, I was surprised to find a sour berry flavor. "What's in here?" I asked.

"It's Oji fruit jam," he said, shoving a full one into his mouth. "They grow in the mountains. Very hard to find."

"It's delicious." I pulled another off. When I bit into it, the jam burst and ran down my chin.

My hands were full, with the stick in one and the container in the other.

Before I could process, Zarios reached over and ran his finger over my chin, collecting all the jam. My cheeks burned as he brought that hand to his mouth and licked it clean off.

"Wouldn't want it to go to waste," he said with a wink.

I laughed and we continued to walk. There was a store at the end selling jewelry, and I couldn't help but think of my sisters. "Can we go there?" I asked.

"We can go wherever you'd like." Zarios looked past me for a moment. "Actually, can I meet you there in a moment? I have a stop to make."

"Sure."

I perused the different pendants and earrings, looking for something to catch my eye. The first I saw was a pair of earrings with a small paint palette on each. It made me think of Sybil. Not many knew, but Sybil used to be an excellent painter. I wasn't sure if she'd made anything since we were children, but she was talented.

It took me a bit longer, but I finally found something for Sage. It was a necklace with sunflowers along the chain. She kept a garden she was very fond of, and I thought she would love this.

I was about to check out when I noticed a small, ornate dagger. The hilt had a large red gem sitting in the middle with black metal filigree around it. It made me think of Zarios. Though it was a bit silly, I threw it on the counter and had the woman bag it up.

By the time I paid, Zarios was back with a small bag in hand. "What's that?" I asked.

"Nothing you need to worry about."

I wanted to press, but I let him have his secret. I had mine after all.

We stopped in a few more stores, not looking for anything in particular. Zarios picked up a few skeins of hand dyed wool for his mother, who he told me liked to knit.

"What's she like?" I asked as we walked.

He looked wistful for a moment. "My mother has always been stern but kind. She wanted me to succeed, and she always did everything she could to see me do so."

I smiled. "That sounds nice."

He nodded. "It seemed your mothers were similar."

I scoffed. "Not really. They want me to do what they want."

"How do you mean?" he asked.

"The whole reason I'm here is to prove I'm not just a soft princess. Since I was old enough to hold a wooden sword, I knew I wanted to be a part of the knights. I had to fight for years to even apply, and they did everything they could to stand in my way of passing."

I always wished my parents would be supportive of me. I knew they probably wanted to protect me, but I wasn't a child anymore. I didn't want to be protected.

He looked thoughtful for a moment. "Though it may be selfish, I'm glad these events brought us both here. You've been an invaluable ally."

My cheeks pinked. His words made me think he really wouldn't take back those from earlier. "Do you think we should head back to prepare for tonight?"

He sighed. "I suppose." I followed his gaze to the horizon. "Why don't we watch the sunset for a moment? We have some time."

I nodded. He took my hand and led us to the edge of the pier. I sat on the side, my feet dangling over the water and my arms resting on the rail, as Zarios plopped down next to me. The sky was a beautiful mix of oranges, blues, and purples. You could see one of the moons already starting to appear, its small, pink form showing just on the horizon. The other moon would come out once it was fully dark. That one was larger and bluer in hue. There was some children's story about them, but I couldn't recall it now.

Seagulls flew across the coast, preparing for the night ahead. The water glittered as waves foamed to the shore. The ocean was beautiful, and I was glad I was here, seeing it for the first time I could remember with Zarios.

I leaned my head against his shoulder. I wasn't sure why, but in this moment, everything else felt a million miles away. It was as if there wasn't a traitor to stop or a knight ship to enter. There was only us and the sunset.

"Is this okay?" I asked.

His arm came around me, pulling me closer. "Yeah, Princess. It is."

Soon, the sun was hidden behind the horizon and the larger moon appeared. "We should probably go," I said.

He squeezed me briefly before standing and holding out his hand.

I took it and held on the whole walk back.

Chapter Twenty-Three

ZARIOS

We prepared for the night the same way we had before. I wore my ornamental armor that dug into my sides and Sorcha changed into a bright red dress with gems down the bodice. Something about seeing her in red set me ablaze.

That was probably why I purchased that red rope sitting in the small bag, tucked into my belongings. I'd seen the fishing supply store and knew they'd carry some.

When I walked in, I pretended to peruse for other things, though the old fisherman behind the counter paid me no mind, his nose in a newspaper.

I walked to the wall, and my eyes caught the bright red rope. I ran my hand over it. It was soft, so it wouldn't chafe her delicate skin.

I took it to the counter. The man took my money without a word.

Now I could only think about tying her up with it. It seemed she would enjoy it too after what happened in the dressing room. I was serious about what I said. After talking to Naram this morning and hearing her tell me how I hurt her, I knew I'd messed up. Though I didn't know where we'd be left when this was all over, I couldn't think about that. I would focus on the now and worry about the rest later.

"Ready?" I asked, putting my arm out.

She took it with ease. Something shifted between us, and I found I didn't mind it.

Mertis had the grandest ballroom, with navy blue walls and tablecloths and gold accessories. All these events were the same. There would be dinner, drinking, dancing, but at least with Sorcha here, I had some form of entertainment.

Dinner happened without much fanfare, and so did the drinking. We had let ourselves get a bit tipsy, but I was less on edge. Though we weren't able to go through every file like we had before, my gut told me it wasn't Naram. That only left one more suspect. I had assumed it could be Prator from the beginning, but I had no proof. I still needed to go in with an objective eye, but he was looking to be our best bet.

I swept her out to the dance floor, and we moved around easily. I saw Naram around with a gray minotaur but had lost Damyr in the crowd. I had seen him near the bar, so he was probably still that way.

As we swayed to a slower song, something began to feel wrong. Looking around, nothing had changed, but the air felt tense, as if something was about to happen.

Then, I saw one man enter who I hadn't seen before. I didn't think anything of it at first, not until I noticed he was underdressed. Then came another, walking the wall, as if he wanted to avoid being seen.

I was about to tell Sorcha when I heard yelling from the doors. They soon burst open, and minotaurs with masks covering their face barged in. They weren't quite masquerade masks, but they had a similar shape, and were all black.

At first, no one noticed, but I stopped. "What?" Sorcha asked, following my gaze. "Shit," she mumbled under her breath, pulling her dagger from her waistband.

"Everyone, to the back exits," I yelled, my voice echoing over the music, which ground to a halt.

One of the men from the group cut through a guest nearest the door, and they dropped to the floor with a thud. People who saw heeded my words, rushing towards safety. Guards rushed the men, but there were many of them.

We jumped into the fray, taking them out left and right. I kept near Sorcha. Though I knew she could hold her own, I couldn't let anything happen to her. I saw Naram to the side, fighting his own group.

I had no idea how they'd gotten in or where they'd come from. As I took another one down, I ripped the cloth off his face. There was no recognition there, just another faceless drone.

We continued fighting our way through. Two of them tried to rush me at once, but I dodged one and let him run into the other, throwing them both to the ground before I took my sword to them both. When I looked back to Sorcha, she had picked up a sword, probably from one of the fallen, and was battling another. Though the sword was obviously heavier than what she was used to, she used it with two hands and easily held her own.

When I found Naram, I realized he was fighting three at once, a battle he seemed to be quickly losing.

"Watch out!" I called as a fourth one aimed for him, swinging his sword right for his head.

Naram ducked out of the way at the last minute, and I jumped into the action, slashing through the man who'd almost killed my friend with little remorse. Though I didn't enjoy killing, I did it when necessary, or when my people were threatened.

A few tried to run once they realized how outnumbered they were but were quickly taken down. The sounds of swords slashing and people yelling filled the room. Chaos was descending, and we needed to get a hold of it.

Luck was on our side. They seemed ill-prepared, and we managed to take them out rather quickly. When the carnage was over, I'd managed to keep one alive. He was slumped in the corner, knocked unconscious.

"Take him to the dungeon," I instructed one of the guards. He nodded, taking him away.

The ballroom was a bloody mess, red smeared against the blue stone floor. A celebration that was meant to be cheerful was turned upside down, and I would ensure whoever planned it would end up just like their men.

As everything wound down, I realized I had lost sight of her. "Sorcha!" I called, worried the worst had happened.

"I'm here," I heard. I followed the voice to the foyer, where she stood over a body. I ran to her, checking her over for wounds.

"Are you hurt?" I asked. There was blood everywhere, making it hard to tell.

"No," she said, out of breath, "but I found this." She held up a small scrap that looked to be an armband of some kind. On the edge was a symbol I didn't recall. It looked like a strange stack of triangles with horns fashioned in the middle.

"Do you know what it means?" she asked.

I shook my head. "I've never seen it before, let's hold onto it. There was one I managed to keep alive for questioning."

"Alright," she said. "Lead the way."

I grabbed her shoulder. "I would prefer it if you went to our rooms."

Her brow furrowed. "What?"

"I will conduct the questioning. You go clean up."

"No," she insisted. "I'm coming with you."

"You can't." I couldn't let her see what I was about to do. Knight or not, I didn't want her to look at me any differently. "Please, just listen."

Hurt flashed in her expression. I was about to explain, but Damyr came around the corner. "Is everyone okay?" he asked.

"Fine. Where were you?"

"As soon as the fighting started, I helped get people to safety. It seemed it was handled on the fighting front."

I nodded. "That was probably for the best. Could you take Sorcha back to our rooms then meet me downstairs?"

"Don't bother," she spit. "I can manage the walk alone." She turned on the balls of her feet and stomped off.

As we moved to the dungeon, I was glad Damyr didn't ask about Sorcha. I wished to follow her, to make sure she was okay. From what she said, this seemed to be her first time in true combat. I was worried about her, but I needed to question the prisoner as soon as possible. We needed all the information we could get from him, it could be the key to ending this. Our safety, and the safety of my kingdom had to come first.

When we got to the bottom of the stairs, Naram was there. His expression was hard, one I rarely saw. "We need to talk," he said to me.

I nodded. "Damyr, why don't you go ahead?"

"Of course. I'll try to wake him."

When Damyr left, Naram pulled me to the side. "I'm assuming what you're dealing with doesn't only have to do with common thieves."

It wasn't a question, but I nodded the same. "It's what we thought at first, but now, I'm sure it's some rebel group."

"And you thought it best not to tell any of us?"

I stayed quiet. Understanding dawned on him. "You think it's a Clarak?"

I again didn't answer. "You thought it could be me?" he sounded hurt.

"I didn't know what to think," I admitted. "I still don't. They've never attacked a location before. It has always been caravans. They're progressing, and if I don't stop them, I'll have a full rebellion on my hands. Someone attacked a shipment of magestones. It had to be someone on the inside, someone who wants me gone."

He sighed. "I understand your predicament, but no, I would never betray you."

I clapped him on the shoulder. "I know you wouldn't. And I never truly suspected, I just had to be sure."

"So what now?"

"Now, we hope this guy has information. And if not, I keep digging."

"Right. Let me know if there's anything I can do. Damyr and I are always on your side. And your intended now as well, who's surprisingly talented with a blade. I must hear her story sometime."

I smiled. "Thank you, brother."

"Uh, Zar," I heard Damyr call from the other room.

Naram and I rushed in. The captive was tied to the chair, his eyes wide and his head tipped back.

"What the fuck happened?" I asked.

I went to him. As soon as I got close enough, I smelled it. Deathwort.

"It seemed it was embedded in his cheek," Damyr said. "As soon as he woke up and realized where he was, he bit down and..." He trailed off, gesturing.

Moons, this wasn't what we needed. "Dispose of him," I said.

"Where are you going?" Naram asked.

"To apologize," I said, taking the stairs three at a time.

CHAPTER TWENTY-FOUR

SORCHA

I SLAMMED THE DOOR to the room, my hands shaking. Blood coated them, as it did my face and body.

I knew there would be blood. Of course, there would be blood, but knowing it and seeing it were two different things. Though I'd done everything to prepare for combat, nothing could have truly prepared me for it. It wasn't even that I was upset about the killing, it just felt...different than I could have ever expected.

I sat, staring at the sword I'd found. It was on the ground next to one of the fallen men. I was toe-to-toe with one of them, and when I blocked with the small dagger, I was sent to the ground. I'd managed to get the other sword in my hand before he struck again, parrying him away. It was heavier than my blade, but it worked all the same.

I stood there, going over it again and again. My adrenaline was fading quickly. Not only that, but I was left out of the interrogation. This fight proved what I could handle, and he still cast me aside. My fists balled in anger.

The door opened. On instinct, I picked up the blade, getting ready to attack anyone coming through. Zarios stood there, hands out.

I dropped the sword. "Sorry," I said. "I'm a bit on edge."

"We all are." His metal breastplate had blood smeared across it. None of it could be seen against his dark fur, but I was sure he was covered the same way I was.

"I'm going to shower," I said. Now that the initial fear was gone, I was still mad.

"Wait." He grabbed my arm, and I let him, looking right at him. "I didn't tell you to leave because I don't trust you or your abilities."

His words surprised me, but I held firm. "Then why did you? I thought you weren't changing your mind anymore?"

"I'm not," he said. "It's because I'm not. I didn't want you to see me that way."

I cocked my head. "What way?"

"I was prepared to torture that man," he said honestly. "I would have done anything to get the information to end all of this. I didn't want you to see me as a monster afterward. None of it matters, though. He managed to off himself before we even got the chance."

I could feel my anger evaporate. "I wouldn't have," I said honestly. "I'm sure my mothers and even maybe my sister have made hard choices, even bad choices, for the good of Peradona, and I'd never hold it against them."

"Yes, but seeing and knowing are different."

"I understand," I said. "But we're partners. Equals. I don't want to be left out. I will never think differently of you."

He looked at me for a long time, or maybe only a few seconds. I only realized when he came at me, pulling me into a heated kiss that I melted into.

"We should shower," I said against his lips. Though his kiss was nice, the blood between us was sticky, making me uncomfortable.

"I agree." He lifted me, hands under my thighs to hold me up. He carried us into the bathroom and set me down before running the water. He undressed, his metal armor clinking to the hard ground.

His muscular body was gorgeous. I could have stared for days.

His hands reached for the tie holding the top together. "May I?"

"Yes."

He peeled it from me, tossing it with his own clothes until we both stood naked. He helped me in, and the water came down, not too hot, not too cold. I scrubbed myself, ready to get rid of all the blood.

Zarios scrubbed himself clean before stepping into the spray to rinse off.

I reached for the soap, but Zarios held it out of reach. He lathered his hands before working them over my shoulders, down each of my arms, scrubbing the grime away with each pass.

"I haven't been bathed since I was a child," I said.

His hands moved to my chest, down my belly. My breath caught when he rubbed over my cunt for a moment before scrubbing my thighs all the way down to my feet. Seeing him kneel in front of me had me hot in the best way.

He stood and added more soap before telling me to turn. When I did, he scrubbed my hair, running his fingers through the strands. My eyes closed. It was so relaxing.

"Rinse," he instructed when he felt I was clean enough. I stepped under the water, letting all the soap and grime wash away down the drain, leaving this whole night behind.

When I was done, I turned the water off. Zarios stepped out, grabbing the towel and passing it to me. I wrapped it around myself before stepping out.

There wasn't a mat on the floor, and I slipped, almost falling on the floor. Zarios managed to catch me easily, though my towel fell to the ground.

"You know, Princess, for a knight, you're a bit clumsy."

"Shut up," I said, shoving him lightly, though there was no real malice behind my words. In truth, I wasn't clumsy, at all. Even before I was a knight, I'd always been steady on my feet. But something about being around this man threw me off balance.

He set me on the counter, the cool stone pressing against my behind. He fit his body against mine, sliding between my thighs. I could feel his heavy cock against my thigh.

"You are gorgeous," he said, his voice hoarse.

My throat choked up a bit at that. I'd been called pretty before, but that wasn't really my thing. I'd never wanted to be seen as attractive. I thought it was a weakness. But having this man find me attractive and powerful at the same time didn't make me feel weak. It made me feel unbreakable.

He brought his lips to mine in a searing kiss. My eyes fluttered closed as his tongue licked across my mouth. I opened for him and let him taste me. Something about this kiss felt different. It felt real.

Zarios wasted no time, dropping to his knees in front of me and spreading my thighs. Seeing this powerful man kneel for me, for *my* pleasure, was its own wet dream.

He planted kisses from one of my knees up my thigh. I ran my hand through his hair, savoring the feeling. The anticipation ramped up as he reached the top of my inner thighs. I could feel how wet he made me.

Instead of going where I wanted, he kissed the crease where my thigh ended and moved to the other knee.

I whined as he started all over again, kissing slowly up my leg. He let out a dark chuckle. "Patience, Princess. I'll give you what you need."

I grabbed hold of his horns, hoping to use them as a guide. Unfortunately, he was in full control of this ride, and I was just along for it.

His pace was painfully slow as he reached the top insides of my thighs. The skin was so sensitive, each touch sent shivers down my spine.

He finally kissed the seam of my thigh and moved to stare at my center. "Moons, this pussy is perfection."

He ran a single finger through me, the wet sound filling the space around us. I let out a small sigh of relief, finally getting what I needed.

"I could live between these thighs," he said. "I would never tire of this taste." He ran his tongue from my opening all the way up to the top.

He sucked my clit in his mouth hard before moving back down to my opening. The way he fucked me with his tongue made me yearn for something different, something bigger.

I held his horns tighter, moaning in pleasure. One of his hands reached up to pluck at my nipple, and the sensation went right down to my clit, sending me careening towards my release.

He moved back up to my clit and quickly replaced his tongue with his fingers. He plunged two in, stretching me impossibly wide.

"Zarios!" I cried his name like he was my deity.

"Fuck, you're tight. I'll need to stretch you to take me."

And I wanted that. I wanted him to take me. A few more circles around my clit was all it took, and I was free falling through my pleasure. My whole body caught ablaze, leaving nothing behind but my need for him.

When I came back down, I released Zarios' horns and fell back against the vanity.

He stood, towering over me, before he lifted me into his arms and carried me to bed, laying me down gently. His silhouette was illuminated by the moons' light, making him look almost ethereal.

His fingers circled me again. "If I'm going to fit, I need you to come for me again." It was as if he'd figured me out already. With only a few strokes, pleasure was rushing through me, throwing me over the edge.

"Good girl," he purred.

He buried his fingers in me and gathered my wetness before slathering it all over his length. I was ready for him, I needed him. Though it had only been a short time, it felt like we'd been through so much together, and I was ready to take this next step with him, ready to let him have me in all the ways I wanted.

"Ready, Princess?" he asked, lining himself up. His thick tip roamed over my cunt, making me feel empty. I needed him to fill me.

"Moons, yes."

Zarios began to gently glide his length into me. It felt as if it would be impossible to fit. He was stretching me more than I thought I could be. He pulled out and eased back in, fitting a bit more each time. My whole body broke out in a light sheen of sweat as my fingers dug into his shoulders, scratching beneath the fur.

He got to the ridge in the middle, and my breath caught. I could feel not only the bar to his piercing, but also the ridge of his cock. I tensed instinctually.

"Relax for me," he said. "I promise not to hurt you."

I brought my hand up against his cheek. "I trust you."

He bent down and kissed me, distracting me enough to enter me further. The ridge went in with a slight pop, and he covered my moan with his kiss as he pushed the rest of the way in.

I felt when he bottomed out, his large balls slapping against my ass. He let out a sated huff I'd yet to hear. "You feel incredible," he said, his voice wobbly.

We sat there like that for a moment, letting me adjust to his size. When I felt comfortable, I shifted experimentally. His ridge rubbed against my g-spot with no effort. Moons, this was going to be good.

"Can I move?" he asked.

I nodded, biting my lip. "Please fuck me."

He growled and pulled out to his ridge before slamming back in. My hands flew to his back, clawing at it. Each time, he got a little faster, fucking me a little harder.

The feeling was addicting.

He held onto my thighs, keeping them spread as he took me how he wanted. "You're so fucking tight, Princess," he said. "I have never known pleasure as good as this."

The mouth on this minotaur was going to be my end.

He fucked into me so hard, the bed began hitting the wall, the sound filling the room between our moans.

"I'm so close," I cried out.

His moved to my clit, circling it perfectly. It felt as if we were in perfect sync, reading each other's bodies and bringing us closer together.

"I want to come inside you," he said. "I want to see you round with my calves."

That statement came out of nowhere. I expected it to throw me off balance, but instead, I found it strangely enticing. The image of him claiming me in every way had me careening closer to the edge. His mouth found my nipple and finished me. My insides tightened around him impossibly more, and I was soaring through the stars.

"Yes, Princess, milk my cock." Zarios continued thrusting into me with abandon until he thrust once more and filled me. I could feel his cum coating my insides, stretching me slightly.

He rocked back and forth, emptying himself fully until I felt the cum trickle out of me.

Zarios flopped down and rolled us to the side, my head resting on his arm. I cuddled into him, pushing his still-hard cock in more. I gasped at the further intrusion.

"Moons, what have you done to me?" he said.

I smiled. "I was just thinking the same thing."

I nuzzled into his chest, embracing his warmth. I could feel myself getting dangerously close to sleeping, but I knew I should get up and clean off.

"If you want," he said, "we could stay like this."

I opened my eyes. "Together?" I asked.

He nodded. "Only if you want."

Did I want it? He felt so good inside me, and the thought of disconnecting from him was a hard thought. I pushed down on him a bit, loving how full he made me. "I want."

He wrapped me in his arms. "Goodnight, Princess."

"Goodnight."

CHAPTER TWENTY-FIVE

ZARIOS

WHEN I WOKE THE next morning, Sorcha was in the same spot I left her. I ran my hand over her raven hair, taking in her clean, earthy scent.

I went to roll and realized my cock was still inside her. Though it was mostly soft, my ridge kept it in place. Being inside of her was the closest I'd ever felt to the After. Every part of my being felt awakened by this woman. I didn't know what it meant for the future, but I didn't know how easily I'd be able to let her go afterwards.

I pulled out a slight bit and pushed back in, testing the waters. My cock hardened quickly, needing to rut her.

"Sorcha," I said lightly, hoping not to wake her fully. Something about using her this freely sent pleasure spiraling through me.

She moaned, the sound making my cock twitch inside of her. "Can I have you?" I asked.

Her eyes cracked a fraction. "Zarios?" she said.

I dropped a kiss to her forehead, and her lashes fluttered shut once again. "Can I fuck you, Princess?"

She squirmed around a bit. "Yes," she said clearly.

I kissed her forehead before thrusting out of her slowly. I buried myself once again, feeling her tight cunt squeeze around me. Every time I pushed into her, it felt like coming home.

She moaned lightly but didn't stir any more. Something about her being so out of it turned on part of my brain I didn't know existed, but I sort of liked it.

One I should be ashamed of, but I relished now, the same way I did in the tailors. The thrill of getting caught washed over me in the same way.

I lashed my tongue over her breast before sucking the pointed tip into my mouth. She tasted like a dream, an addiction no drug could compete with.

I needed her to come for me like I needed my next breath. She did nothing but moan slightly, her breath picking up a bit, as if she was dreaming of me.

I circled her clit the way she liked, the way I knew I could get her off. She let out a loud moan as I felt her walls tighten, strangling my cock.

I felt a tingling at the base of my spine. A few more thrusts, and my balls drew up as I came deep inside of her. I groaned low, feeling her pussy milk me for everything I had. And I would give it all up easily.

When I finished, I pulled all the way out of her, watching my cum drip from her cunt. I ran my finger through it, through our shared release.

"There are much less dirty ways to say good morning," she mumbled.

I gazed up, and she was looking over at me. I pushed up and dropped my lips to hers. "But I prefer the dirty way."

She smiled. "I think I do as well."

"Let's wash up. We need to get going early this morning."

She groaned, rolling over into the pillow. "Fine, but you need to carry me. Someone put my legs out of commission."

I laughed low and swept her out of bed, carrying her bridal style. It made me think of this being reality. Carrying her like this across the threshold of our home. Giving her everything she's ever desired. It seemed like such a faraway possibility, but at the same time, it felt like something attainable. Maybe we could have this. I *wanted* this, I realized. The thought came so suddenly, it almost scared me, but I was having a hard time pushing it away.

We washed up quickly and dressed for the trip. Though last night was perfect, we still had a job to finish. I hoped to find the proof I needed easily and put an end to all of this.

Sorcha wore a pair of green flowy pants, a white tunic tucked into the waistline. Though I wanted her to wear what she was comfortable in, I couldn't deny my love for seeing her in pants. They hugged her curves just right, giving me a better look at everything.

When we arrived at the foyer, Naram was there, along with Damyr and Kiaza.

"Sir," Kiaza greeted. "Do you still plan to move forward with the tour?"

I cocked my head. "Why wouldn't we?"

She looked to Damyr. "We just thought it may be safer to head back. I'm sure Prator would understand with these circumstances."

I kept my face neutral, but her words sent alarm bells off in my head. Was there another reason she was keeping us away?

"What do you think, Damyr?" I asked.

He shrugged. "Whatever decision you make, my men and I will keep you safe."

Naram scoffed. "It was a close call last night."

"Because your guards were caught off guard," Damyr defended. "If they were better prepared, it wouldn't have happened."

Naram turned to him. "My guards were outnumbered. Many of their lives were lost. How dare you—"

"Okay," I cut in. "Kiaza, I appreciate your concern, but we will be continuing. Please send all the other advisors back. We will make the journey alone. Send half of the guards with them."

Her eyes widened. "Are you sure, sir? We don't want to leave you and your intended unprotected."

"Half of the guards are plenty for the journey. Get my advisors back safely. We will finish the trip and deal with everything when we get to Ashmore."

She cast her eyes down, scribbling in her book. "Understood."

Her hooves clicked as she scurried away to complete my orders. Naram and Damyr were still in a starring match.

I clapped them each on the shoulder, drawing their attention. "I know this was hard, but anyone could have done one thing differently to stop it. If we turn on each other, they win."

They looked back to each other. "You're right," Naram sighed first. I was surprised. He was normally the more bullheaded one, unwilling to apologize.

"I apologize," Damyr said. "I should have respected your losses more."

This moment reminded me of us as younglings. I always had the coolest demeanor. Damyr would fly off the handle at a moment's notice, and Naram was so stubborn, he would never let things go. I was always the mediator between them, though back then, our biggest issue was who had the most rock skips or who drank the most the night before.

How things had changed.

"As expected, I accept Sorcha Yulean as our Grand Clarak's intended mate," Naram said. "May you prosper in your marriage."

I hugged him. "Thank you, brother."

"Of course. You take care of her. She knows I'll always be waiting," he said with a wink.

I smacked him upside the head. He laughed, and so did Sorcha.

"It's not funny," I grumbled.

Sorcha took my hand. "It's a little funny."

Soon after, we packed up to go. The other council members were loaded up, headed back home on the quickest route.

"Everything's ready," Damyr said. "The trip should only take the day if we don't stop for breaks."

We decided on lesser known and closed routes, hoping to avoid any more trouble.

Sorcha had her nose buried in one of the other books she'd stolen from my room. Though I preferred being up and moving, it felt like I could sit perfectly still for hours, just watching her. Her eyes ran across each page, a slight crinkle sitting between her brows.

I never thought I'd feel this way, not even about an intended mate I chose without the pressures of a ruse. I couldn't help but worry she didn't feel the same. Though she'd said she didn't want me to take it back, that didn't mean she wanted to actually be my intended, and this didn't seem like the most opportune time to ask. But when everything was over and we arrested the ones responsible, where would that leave us? I wanted to ask her to stay with me, but could I give her what she wanted? Though I believed in her abilities fully, could I give her a position on the guard, knowing I was willingly putting my mate at risk?

But if I sent her back, she would become one anyway. Not only would she be at risk, but she would no longer be mine. The push and pull of it made my head spin, but I would need to figure it out sooner rather than later. I *would* figure it out. There was no other option. To keep Valcor safe, we needed to solve this, and then I would tell her how I truly felt.

"There!" Sorcha said loudly, snapping me from my daze.

"What?" I asked.

She had her finger pointed to the page. "I thought that symbol looked familiar. The one we found on that guy. I had thumbed through this book a bit, but I didn't spend much time looking at it."

I glanced under at the cover. *The History of War in Valcor.*

She turned the page to me, and my eyes widened. It was the same symbol he wore. I read the passage below the symbol.

The Inika is a symbol representing strength and the desire to retrieve what one is owed. It tells your opponent they've wronged you in some way and that you're out for revenge. The only options are success or death. There will be no middle ground. It ends when the avenged is satisfied.

I read the passage twice, stunned. "I don't understand," I said. "I can think of no one I've wronged in this way."

She read the passage again, chewing on her lip in thought. "Maybe it's a perceived slight, one you had no idea you were committing."

"Maybe," I agreed. "But this feels drastic. I have no clue how I would wrong someone this impactfully without knowing it."

She shrugged. "Or the person just wants power. Maybe they feel they deserve it and are just taking it out on you."

I pondered that. It was a possibility, but it all felt too pre-meditated for that.

"I have something to say," Sorcha interrupts. "Unrelated."

She set the book aside, and I gave her my full attention. "I know that we haven't talked about what happens...after, but no matter what does, I'm not ready for a kid. I took my yearly tonic to avoid pregnancy, and I have no interest in having kids any time soon. Maybe never."

I cocked my head, unsure where this was coming from. Then, my words from last night dawned on me. "I apologize," I said. "I shouldn't have said that without discussing it with you. I agree. I'm not sure where we're headed, but I have no plans to bring a child into this world any time soon."

Her eyes widened. "But you said—"

I know," I interrupted, not wanting to hear her repeat it. My tail swished against the seat behind me. "I understand your confusion. The truth is, in the moment, I just enjoy the idea of it. It...gets me off more. But I shouldn't have said it without discussing it with you. I apologize."

Her entire face was now red. "It's fine. I must admit, I kind of liked it too. I've liked everything we've done. I just wanted to be on the same page."

"I understand. We should probably go over boundaries at some point, but for now, we should implement a safe word."

"Safe word?" she asked.

I nodded. "It's a word either of us can use to let the other know we want to stop. It stops whatever's happening, and we can either talk about it and continue or stop all together and figure out what went wrong."

I watch the wheels turning. "Doesn't 'stop' do?"

I smiled. "In most cases, yes, but with the way you like receiving pain and the way I like giving it, you may not always mean it. It should be a word that wouldn't come up during sex."

If I held up a tomato, it would disappear against her skin. "Got it." She thought some more. "What about turnip?"

I quirked my brow. "Turnip?"

"Yes, they're quite bad. It will kill the mood quickly."

I laughed. "Turnip it is."

CHAPTER TWENTY-SIX

SORCHA

WE ARRIVED TO THVETHARION that night. Unlike the bright blues of Mertis and the leafy greens of Sobury, Thvetharion was all gray. Each building was made from colored stone, with large chimneys coming out of most. I recall reading Thvetharion did a lot of blacksmithing, not only providing weapons, but pans, utensils, anything you could think of. Even still, it all felt a bit drab.

Their castle wasn't much better. It was stone, with four watchtowers surrounding the four corners. I could see minotaurs sitting up there, crossbows at the ready. I leaned into Zarios. "They seem welcoming," I said.

He huffed. "Very."

When we stopped, Zarios got out first and helped me out. I took his hand and stepped down. There were a few minotaurs scattered around, all in leather armor, save for one. He had a light brown coat and short cut fringe. His eyes were worn on the sides, crinkling from age.

"Welcome, Grand Clarak Zarios," he said. He didn't even move to bow.

My eyes moved to Zarios, who didn't seem surprised. "Clarak Prator," he said. "Thank you for hosting. We appreciate the invitation."

"I appreciate you following the proper order of things," he said. His tone indicated it was a slight, but I wasn't sure how. "And this must be your intended?"

"Yes, Princess Sorcha Yulean," he introduced.

"A pleasure," I said, though the words felt like a lie.

"A human has a lot to prove here," he said to Zarios, talking as if I wasn't standing right there.

"Well, this human is perfectly comfortable doing so," I said pointedly.

I saw amusement glimmer in Zarios' eyes, but no such thing was found with Prator. "We will see. Come, get settled."

We followed him in. The place was dark and dreary, black chandeliers hanging from the ceilings but nothing else, not a painting to be found anywhere. There were almost no windows or any other source of light.

When we got to the rooms, they were the same, a single bed with dark sheets and a side table greeted us. "They seem more hospitable by the minute," I said, flopping onto the bed.

Zarios listened at the door for a moment before he rushed me. "I know this sounds outlandish, but I'm sure it's Prator."

I snorted. "You think? This whole place reads like an evil lair. But why didn't you tell me this before we left?"

He laughed darkly. "I wanted you to meet him before I gave you any preconceived notions. I wanted your initial reaction. I know we're used to sneaking around, but I want to find whatever evidence we can and leave as soon as possible."

I nodded. For a moment, I worried he was leaving me out again, but his thought process made sense. "Then we'll have to be a bit more cunning," I said. A plan formed in my mind. It may have been a ridiculous one, but it was one that could work.

"I've got it."

"I still don't like this," Zarios said as he buckled his pants.

"Too bad," I said, hooking my larger dagger to my belt. I was meant to go totally unseen, so it didn't matter if I had it out.

"Go," I insisted. "I will be fine."

He grabbed my hand and pulled me in for a quick kiss I wasn't expecting. "Come back in one piece, Princess," he said.

"Always."

With that, he left. I paced the room, nerves getting the best of me. I knew what I had to do. While Zarios went to speak with Prator, I would go to his office and find what we needed. There had to be some correspondence that would nail him. He was our last bet.

After about ten minutes, I had to assume it was safe. I slipped out and made my way to his office. Zarios had spent the last hour going over a map highlighting every nook and cranny of the castle. I knew the route I would take, and I had a backup if it didn't go to plan. The place was fairly empty, and in these back halls, it was even more silent.

I made it there without any issues. Though the door was locked, I pulled out my dagger and wiggled the lock open. It was only slightly damaged, and by the time someone noticed, we would be gone.

The office was thankfully empty. Compared to everything else, it was extravagant. Expensive art hung on the walls, and everything was lined in gold.

I searched through his drawers, careful to leave everything the way I found it before moving on. I found nothing more than documents about steel prices, a few collectible stamps, and a bottle of lotion next to some tissues that were both too empty for my liking.

I opened the left bottom row and realized the drawer inside appeared slightly smaller than the outside made it look. The only things inside were a few replacement pens and other office supplies. I wiggled around the drawer until I felt a small dent.

When I pulled on it the drawer open, the bottom fell out, and pieces of worn parchment fell from it. I lifted them and began sifting through the pile.

My eyes widened. This was basically a written confession, letters exchanged, talking about their plans and all the money associated. This proved that not only was Prator involved, but he had a partner. He never addressed them directly in the letters, but it would be easy enough to draw them out, though it may mean we stayed here a bit longer.

I slid them into my pack and put the bottom of the drawer back. As I was shutting the door, a key jammed into the lock. I looked around, coming up with a plan. I ran for the closet, closing the door most of the way behind me. It was cracked open when I went in, and I didn't want him to sense anything was off. Luckily, I'd messed the lock up enough to make the key hard to get in but not enough for him to notice, it seemed.

I tucked myself against the dark corner and waited. I even quieted my breathing, making myself undetectable.

"Damn Prator can't even afford a nice lock with all the money I've given him."

The door shut, and I recognized the voice immediately. *Damyr?*

I stayed still as he rummaged a bit. It seemed he wasn't looking for the letters, but something else. Why would he be giving Prator money and shuffling through his office?

"Moons, you idiot," he grumbled to himself. "I give you one simple task, make sure they kill Naram. He couldn't even do that." He continued rummaging. "Fuck!" he shouted to no one. I forced myself not to jump.

"As soon as this bastard helps me end this, I'm ending him. I won't need him once I'm Grand Clarak." I had to suppress my gasp. *Shit.* Damyr was the partner.

"There you are," he said, fishing out something from the drawer. After finding whatever he was looking for, he left, but I saw a flash of him as he went, locking the door behind him.

Fuck, how was I going to tell Zarios?

CHAPTER TWENTY-SEVEN
ZARIOS

MY MEETING WITH PRATOR had finished twenty minutes ago, and there was no sign of Sorcha. I was worried. Had she been caught? I didn't think so. I would have heard it by now.

That meeting was hell. I pretended to be interested in the tax proposition his underling had brought forth months ago. I acted interested to give Sorcha time, asking questions I didn't care about and pretending to consider his underhanded bribe—though with the amount he offered, I couldn't help but wonder where he got it. Though Thvetharion did well, they didn't do that well, even with a greedy leader.

I was thinking of finding her myself when the door clicked open. I was on my feet in a second.

"Did you find anything?" I asked quickly.

Sorcha nodded, her eyes cast down.

"Did he do it?" I asked.

"Yes," she said, her face pinched, "but he had an accomplice."

"An accomplice? That would make sense. It's a big operation, and he's not the brightest. We'll find them eventually." Still, this did change things. If we just took

229

Prator out, his accomplice would probably go into hiding, and I wanted to find them before that.

She swallowed hard, and I knew there was something else.

"What aren't you telling me?" I asked, dread clawing up my throat.

She looked me in my eyes. "You know I would never lie to you, right?"

"I do." And I meant it.

"Okay." She paused for another moment. "I found these letters in a fake bottom of a drawer. I sifted through them briefly, which is when I realized he was working with someone. I thought we would catch them later—until someone walked in."

She averted her gaze again. *Someone I knew.*

I clenched my knuckles. "Who was it?"

"Damyr," she said so quietly, I almost didn't hear it.

"No," I said quickly. "You must be mistaken."

She put her hand on my arm. "I'm so sorry, Zarios. I snuck into the closet and saw him myself. I'm sure you would recognize his handwriting."

She pulled out the letters. I snatched them from her—probably too abruptly—and looked through them.

I read all the words detailing the betrayal. Talking about where to attack and when. Outlining my downfall.

All written in my best friend's handwriting.

I dropped the letters, the parchment scattering below me. Sorcha took me in her arms, and I curled around her, letting her be my strength. Devastation didn't even cover the way I felt. It felt as if my heart was ripped from my chest, a betrayal I couldn't begin to understand.

All the things that had happened slowly started to make sense. His disappearance during the attack, the prisoner we found dead... He was the only one who saw what happened. Even when he'd first come back, I thought he'd seemed different. I thought he'd just gotten better, but it was obvious I was wrong.

I had no clue why he did what he did or how, but I would find out.

Soon.

I pulled away, feeling a slight dampness around my eyes I forced back. I would grieve the friend I thought I had later. Now, we needed a plan.

We went through the motions of the next few days. Prator didn't seem to suspect anything, and neither did Damyr. We attended the ball and pretended everything was fine, even though I was dying inside. Sorcha stayed by my side, giving me small squeezes and glances that told me she felt for me.

After a long discussion that first night, we decided to deal with it back in Ashmore. All Claraks were expected to attend the final mating ceremony, and there would be more room for error there. We weren't sure who else was in on it in Thvetharion, and we couldn't take chances. Though we didn't expect any outward attacks here, it would be too obvious.

To my surprise, Prator easily accepted Sorcha. I wasn't sure if it was to move their plan along and get us out or because he actually found her worthy, but either way, I didn't care. His judgment meant nothing to me.

Last night, I had her write a letter to her mothers, letting them know the situation and telling them to prepare for anything. The letters had no detail, but with his easy acceptance, it was plain to see they had something planned. We had to be ready.

Prator planned to follow our troupe back to the city. I agreed and insisted Damyr stay with Prator. Though he fought it at first, I convinced him they needed extra protection. While it might have been better to have him travel with us, I couldn't stand being so close to him for that long. My hand sat on my blade the entire way back. Luckily, it wasn't too far, and we made it with no issues.

At least in Ashmore, there was more security. Though I still wasn't aware of all the involvement, I knew there would be less than in Thvetharion.

When we arrived, Prator went to settle in, and I instructed Damyr to prepare the guards for the event tomorrow. I counted all of them out anyway, they worked too closely with Damyr to be trusted.

He did as requested, and I ordered Kiaza to find Naram, who'd arrived that morning, and meet us in my office in an hour.

We had time to kill, but I just wanted to lie down. I wanted to bury myself under the blankets and never come out.

"Hey," Sorcha said. I realized I was just staring at a wall. "Follow me."

I took her hand and allowed her to lead me away. She brought me to an abandoned training room. It was old, with outdated mats and weapons on the walls.

"What's this?" I asked.

She passed me a practice sword. "I thought you could use this."

I smiled at her. She took her position, and I matched her. She took the first swing, one I parried easily. We continued the back and forth. Neither of us went all out, just flexing our muscles and practicing a bit.

It got me out of my head, putting my focus on our match. Though we were going easy, I still wished to win.

She faked left and went low, and I almost missed it. I regained focus and struck the right. She easily blocked but was caught off balance by the quick movement.

I saw that as my chance and went for the left. However, this time, she planted her foot firmly and blocked. It was a risky move, and now, I was off balance.

She took advantage, safely sweeping my feet and knocking me over. She moved quickly, tackling me and drawing the fake sword to my throat. Her smile was triumphant.

"Told you I'd take you down," she said proudly.

I couldn't help it. I pulled her in, planting a firm kiss to her lips, and she let me, melting into me.

This woman was becoming my lifeline. One I couldn't go without.

When she pulled away, she asked, "Do you do that with all your sparring partners?"

I laughed for the first time in days. "I would think not. Naram sure wouldn't appreciate that."

She shrugged. "I don't know. He seemed very open-minded."

I rolled quickly, flipping her to her back, sitting over her on my hands. "Thank you," I said against her lips.

"Of course," she said, caressing my face with her hands. "Anything."

Stay.

I wanted to say it, but it didn't feel right. I needed my kingdom to be safe. Then, I would tell her how I felt. I couldn't be sure she would agree to stay, and though that scared the hell out of me, I couldn't miss the chance. After everything that happened, I couldn't just let her go, not without trying.

The fear of her rejection weighed so heavily, it threatened to crush me.

I brought my lips down to hers, trying to tell her without words, but she needed them, deserved them.

"We should probably go," I said, standing and offering her my hand.

She took it easily and held it the whole way to the meeting room.

When we arrived, Naram was there along with Kiaza. "What's happened?" he asked as we entered. "Did you find the culprit?"

I nodded, unable to speak.

"Who is it?"

I cleared my throat, and Sorcha squeezed my hand in comfort. "Prator is involved, which we expected, but..." I pulled the letters out of my bag.

Naram took them, his eyes roaming over each page. I sat down, letting him read. I could tell when he got to the part Damyr wrote, asking for a group to kill Naram. His face pinched with the same pain I felt. Sorcha took the seat next to mine, her eyes filled with empathy.

Kiaza looked over his shoulder, her eyes widening in realization.

"This can't be real," Naram said after a moment.

"I didn't want to believe it either," I said. "But there's hard evidence. He was also the only one unaccounted for during the attack, the only one who saw the prisoner die. It's him."

Naram stood, pacing the floor. "I don't understand. Why would he betray us? Betray you?"

I swallowed. "I have no idea." I gestured for Sorcha to pass me the book, and she did easily. I opened to the page. "The men that night were wearing this symbol." I passed it over to him, his eyes scanning the passage.

"What wrong has been done to him? If anything, we helped the poor bastard before he threw his entire life away."

He chucked the book against the wall so hard, it left a dent.

I stood, resting my hand on his shoulder. "Why?" he whispered.

"I don't know, but we're going to stop him. That's why I brought you in. We need a plan."

He clasped my hand. "Anything, brother."

We shared a moment of understanding. It used to be the three of us, but Damyr was no longer the friend we knew. There would be plenty of time to grieve, but now was time for action.

Sorcha spoke up. "They're probably planning something for tomorrow. Everyone's here, and it's the perfect opportunity to set out whatever goal they had."

I agreed. "I assume they're trying to take me down. Replace me, that's what it sounded like. There can be formal challenges to the Grand Clarak at any time, but it seems neither choose to go that route."

"Probably because they knew they couldn't win," Naram said.

I huffed. "That was my assumption as well, so they need to do something else. Their plans to start a war with other nations have failed thus far, so they had to change tactics. The notes end well before that, so I'm not sure what their next move is."

"Get you to give up by force," Sorcha said. Her eyes were wide, as if she'd figured it all out. "They're trying to target things you care about. Naram, your kingdom...me."

I realized where she was going. "You think they're going to use you as leverage?"

She shrugged. "It's the only thing they have left. If they can use me to get to you, they probably think you'd give up to get me back."

"I would," I said, holding her gaze. "They're right."

She swallowed hard.

"That's not an option," Naram cut in. "So if that's their plan, when would they do it?"

"I would guess tonight," I said. "Intended mates are supposed to spend the night before the final mating alone. It would give them enough time to get you somewhere else before anyone noticed."

"So we need to stop them before that," I said.

"No," Sorcha said.

"No?"

"This is our chance," she said, obviously on a roll. "Even if you arrest them now, whatever faction they have will still be out there. I'm sure they'll take me to whatever hideout they have, and we'll be able to flush them out all at once."

I shook my head. "No. We can't put you at risk."

"I won't be. You'll follow from a safe distance and surprise them, taking them all out."

"It's not a bad idea," Naram said unhelpfully. "I have some trustworthy men we can take, and I'm sure you have a few as well."

I did, and while the logic was sound, I couldn't risk it. I couldn't risk her. "No. It's too dangerous. There has to be another option."

"There's not." She stood, walking over to me. "This is what I came here for. To prove myself. To help save your people. We're running out of time, and this is our best option."

"You don't need to prove yourself to anyone," I said harshly, grabbing her shoulders. "You are an excellent fighter, with a brave heart and a fighting spirit. Anyone with a brain would be lucky to have you on their side. But *I* can't risk you. If something happened, I…" I didn't know what I would do.

Her eyes were wet but determined. "Then it's your job to not let anything happen to me. Though I can hold my own, I know you'll be there to have my back."

I looked to Naram, who kept his face neutral. I knew either decision I made, he would support me. We could come up with something else. But Sorcha was right, this was our best chance.

"Fine," I conceded. "We do it your way. I'll keep you safe."

She leaned into me. "I know."

Chapter Twenty-Eight
SORCHA

THAT NIGHT, I WAS taken to a separate suite to sleep. I wore a bulky pair of sleep pants that could hide a miniature blade easily. I needed to look the part of the damsel, so I didn't carry my sword.

I knew Zarios was hiding in the room next to mine and Naram was stationed outside out of view. Though we were basing this plan on the assumption they would come tonight, I knew in my gut that it would work. I trusted Zarios, and I trusted myself.

I laid down in the bed and rolled over, allowing my breathing to even out and my eyes to close. My nerves ramped up the longer I laid there, but this was what had to be done. I trusted them to keep me safe, and I trusted myself to succeed.

I heard the door click and forced myself to remain where I was. Though I wanted to take out whoever chose to come after me, I needed to allow myself to be taken.

I heard them creep towards the bed, getting closer. I had to fight my instinct to panic. I knew this was coming, though I wanted to fight it.

What I didn't expect was the cloth over my mouth. I reacted, unable to help it. When my eyes flew open, Damyr stood above me.

"Sorry, Princess," he said, holding the sweet-smelling cloth to my face. "It's not personal. And I won't kill you. Don't need Peradona on my bad side when I become Grand Clarak."

You will never become Grand Clarak. I tried to say it, but my lips wouldn't move. I tried to stay awake, but no matter how hard I fought, my eyes dropped closed. Though I should have been scared, I wasn't.

I knew Zarios would save me.

CHAPTER TWENTY-NINE
ZARIOS

I LISTENED THROUGH THE wall, all my concentration on any sounds. I listened as Sorcha pretended to ready for bed. My insides twisted at all the ways this could go wrong. It couldn't. Sorcha would be fine, and we would catch them. If I didn't keep telling myself that, I would feel myself spiral, and that couldn't happen. She needed me.

Once she'd stopped moving, I waited until finally hearing the click of the door. I'd hoped it wouldn't happen, that she was wrong, but she was too smart for her own good.

I couldn't hear what was happening, but I heard when the door clicked once again. I waited a few moments before I ran to the window and gave Naram the signal. He came from the darkness and nodded, heading towards the servants' entrance. Luckily, there were only a few ways to go. We had men stationed outside all of them, just in case, but I had a feeling he would take the servants' corridor in the west wing. It was where we'd go to sneak out as adolescents, and he was a creature of habit.

I took an alternate path to get there and, sure enough, I watched Damyr carry a limp Sorcha. He must have drugged her with something or knocked her out. The thought of him hurting her made me see red, but I had to follow through. I promised Sorcha I would.

I watched them walk the fence line as Naram came from the edge of the building. I silently gestured in that direction, and we went with a nod. We followed them for a while until we hit the forest.

"The old dungeon," I said. "It's the only thing out here."

"You're right. Let me gather the men and come out. Shouldn't be more than a few minutes. Please wait."

I nodded, following way behind so as to not draw any attention. This prison hadn't been operational since before our time. It was the perfect place to have too much to drink and do stupid shit.

He went to the side entrance, where one guard stood and went in, shutting the stone door behind him. Having her out of view was painful, but I knew he wouldn't hurt her. Whatever his plan was, angering Peradona was not a part of it.

I was going to save Sorcha, just like I promised.

CHAPTER THIRTY
SORCHA

MY EYES CRACKED OPEN, greeted by a harsh light. I was lying on something relatively soft, staring up at a single lantern hanging above me. My head spun as I tried to recall what happened.

Right—Damyr kidnapped me. I sat up abruptly and instantly regretted it. My world spun and my stomach turned. I put my head between my knees, trying to ground myself.

"Finally awake," a voice in front of me said. I looked up to find Damyr standing there, his previously kind face looking much different, almost unhinged. He was on the other side of a row of bars, keeping me in. The walls around us were sturdy concrete, but the cell looked decrepit and cracked. If I had to guess, we were in some kind of retired prison.

"What am I doing here?" I asked.

"Just a bit of a bargaining chip, that's all. Sorry to bring you in the middle, but I'm doing what must be done."

"What are you talking about?" I needed to keep him talking, keep him distracted to give Zarios the best chance of finding me.

"I'm assuming Zarios hadn't told you," he said. "He probably feels shame around the whole thing."

I watched him pace as if he was the caged one. "I had the opportunity to become Clarak of Mertis, just like my father had, and his father before."

"I thought it had nothing to do with blood?" I questioned.

He scoffed. "Only children believe that. No commoner could become a Clarak, much less Grand Clarak. That bastard just got lucky."

I didn't believe that but didn't dare say it aloud. "That didn't matter, though," he continued. "Stranger things had happened, and I knew I was going to be Clarak of Mertis. My whole life was set in front of me. With my best friend as Grand Clarak, I had a better chance of being chosen anyway. That was, until those snakes betrayed me. They allowed my father to convince them I had a 'problem'" he air quoted. "As if everyone didn't have their own fun. And to send me away, right before the trials? I was seen as weak. He put Naram up instead, and he took *my* rightful place, that ungrateful *peasant*," he spat. "He has no noble blood to speak of. He doesn't deserve it."

"That's why you attacked in Mertis," I said, all the pieces falling together.

He looked back at me, as if I'd pulled him from his vision. "I hoped to at least take out Naram, but the idiots in my employ couldn't even do that much. I want them both gone, and you're my ticket to do that."

"Why stay by him for all these years?" I asked. "You're his head of guard."

He shrugged. "Keep your enemies close and all that. That pity job when I came back meant nothing. It was a consolation to the power I would have had. I was set up, and now, they'll all pay."

It all made sense—the symbol, the letters... It all fell into place except. "Why bring Prator into it?"

His gaze cut to mine. "I'm not surprised Zarios figured that out. I knew he would eventually. Prator was just an easy way to get men and weapons. That idiot believed I would give him Grand Clarak and happily accept Clarak of Thvetharion. He just hates the progress Zarios is trying to make. I only had to promise the bare minimum to get him to agree."

"And what about the magestones?"

"Ah, that was Prator's only good idea," he said, looking into the distance fondly, like everything he did was a pleasant memory. "We sold off half to fund some of our troops, but we kept some, just in case."

My mouth felt dry. Though we'd figured a lot of it out, some of it was new. I tried to wrap my head around it. "What will you do with me?"

He cocked his head. "Once I get Zarios to hand over his position willingly, I'll have him killed, and you can go back to your lush princess life."

An idea formed in my head, and I smiled. "Good," I said.

His brow quirked. "Good? I'm telling you my plans to kill your intended, and you're pleased?"

I nodded. "Between us, I hate him. He threatened me in Peradona, told me it was the only way to prevent a war, and if I didn't, he would hurt my family. I had no choice."

I let the crocodile tears fall easily. "I'm glad he'll be gone. He has done us both wrong."

A twisted smirk took over his face. Having someone validate his views gave him a rush, which was exactly what I expected. "I knew there was something I liked about you," he said. "And that makes sense. He would do anything for his strange sense of justice."

I sniffled, rubbing my eyes for show. "I knew you were the real brains behind everything when I got here. I just didn't expect you to be *this* smart. I've always wanted a bit of power myself. I saw the way you gazed lingered on my sister. Though I'm not her, you could pretend."

My doe eyes drew him in, hook, line, and sinker. He approached the bars. "Take not only his kingdom, but his woman too? I like the sound of that. Though your sister is much more attractive, I guess you would do."

His words made me want to end him right there, but I needed him to let me out. I stood, glad my head seemed a bit clearer, and moved forward. "Good," I said quietly. "That poor bastard could hardly get it up. I would love him to know a real man had me before he perished."

I let my sleeve slip from my shoulder, dipping my shirt a bit more to reveal the top of my breast.

His eyes caught the movement. He licked his lips. "I think that could be arranged."

He opened the door and stepped in, not bothering to shut it behind him. He approached me, sliding his hand up the side of my face.

I let out a small, fake moan, feeling him up as well. Just as his lips were about to touch mine, I reached for the dagger in my waistband and drove the blade into his side, right into his liver.

He cried out and fell to the ground. I pulled the blade free and wiped it before bounding towards the door. He grabbed my foot, and I fell, the air knocking from my lungs.

I kicked my foot back, crushing him right in his snout. Blood began pouring from it, and he released me, his hands going towards it. I got out and slammed the door shut, locking it.

He reached around himself. "Looking for these?" I asked, holding his key ring up.

His eyes widened. "You stupid bitch! Let me out!" He rushed the door, but I stepped back, watching him struggle.

I leaned in a bit, but not enough to let him grab me. "Never underestimate me."

With that, I walked away, leaving Damyr's screams far behind me.

Time to find Zarios.

CHAPTER THIRTY-ONE

ZARIOS

I SHIFTED ON MY feet, waiting. Naram was taking too long. We needed to move. Unable to help it, I snuck up on the guard near the door, my sword at the ready.

I threw a rock across to his other side. On instinct, he turned to check on the noise, and that was when I struck. I stuck my blade right through the back of his neck where there was a slight seam in the armor.

He froze as I pulled the blade out. He fell to the ground, hands barely making it to his neck before he was dead. The sound of him falling drew no attention, and I slipped in.

It was just as I remembered, dark and falling apart, though now, all the lights were lit, and the floor was at least swept. This must have been where he was planning the entire time.

I walked quietly stalking through the halls. I took out another guard I saw, but the place didn't have the best security. They were probably comfortable in the idea that they wouldn't get caught.

I reached a door with a light streaming through it. I stood for a moment, listening. "I don't care what Damyr said." I recognized it as Prator immediately. "We're going

249

through with the attack. Zarios would never give up his entire kingdom for some woman."

On that, Damyr was correct, but it didn't matter now. "Understood. I'll inform the others."

The guard left, walking down the other side of the hall, missing me completely. I got a bit farther away from Prator's office before I was on him, taking him down with ease.

I left him there in the hall before going to the office and opening the door. "I told you, Xanth, I don't care..." The words died on his tongue as his eyes widened.

"Z-Zarios," he stuttered, coming around the table. "What are you doing here?"

"I was about to ask you the same thing." My fist went flying, wailing into his face.

He screamed, grabbing his snout. "I was wondering why one of my loyal Claraks participated in this plan to overthrow me."

His eyes widened. "Sir, it's not... Damyr, he—"

"I know all about Damyr," he said. "And I know about you. I suspected you originally, but I knew an imbecile like you could do this alone."

Anger marred his features. "You're the imbecile. You're trying to change traditions this nation has always held dear, and for what?"

"For the good of everyone!" I snapped. "Not just those at the top."

He scoffed. "Your father would be ashamed of you."

I landed another blow to his face. "My father was a general who stood up for what he believed in."

I drew my sword, and his eyes widened further as he tried to back up, hitting the wall behind him. "I—I meant no harm. Please!"

"Where's my intended?" I said, holding him by the chest, my sword at his throat.

He swallowed, long and deep. "The dungeon below. I swear, she's alive."

I smiled. "Glad to know one of you will be."

He went to say something else, but I didn't let him. My sword sliced through him like butter, and I dropped him to the ground. His hand went to his bubbling throat, but his eyes stayed open.

After a moment, he stopped flailing and went still, the puddle around him growing by the second.

I left the room and headed to the stairs. One man was shouting, probably finding one of the bodies I left behind.

I moved quickly, taking the stairs two at a time. When I rounded the corner, I bumped into a small figure in front of me.

I drew my sword but quickly stopped when I saw my little mate with a sword of her own. She ran to me, jumping into my arms. I caught her, bringing her lips to mine.

"How did you get out?" I asked.

She laughed, kissing me once more. "Haven't you learned by now not to underestimate me?"

I heard more shouting from above, along with the sounds of fighting. "Naram and his men are here."

She nodded. "He's in there if you wanted to see him."

I looked down the hall. With a big breath, I forced myself to move in that direction. I slowed when I got to the cell he was in. He was bleeding from his side, which was how I assumed my mate got herself out.

I readied my blade when I heard someone rushing around the corner, but I lowered it as Naram came into view. "We've cleared most of them out."

His eyes fell to Damyr.

When he looked up at me, he spit in our direction, unable to move.

I squatted in front of the bars, taking him in. "Why?" It came out as a whisper.

His eyes narrowed. "You ruined me. I was going to be Clarak of Mertis before you took it from me."

"What are you talking about?" I asked.

With his last ounce of energy, he flung himself at the bars. "*I* was next in line. My father told you I needed help because he hated me. He wanted to see me fail, and he sent me away right before the trials. It wasn't a coincidence. He saw me as weak and refused to give me my *rightful* place. It was all because you let him take it from me!"

I stood there, stunned. "You were going to drink yourself to death before you even stepped in the arena. We spent three days tracking you down after one of your benders, and we found you about to attack a woman. You were out of control."

"I would have handled it!" he screamed.

I pushed him down, feeling satisfied as he smacked against the ground. "We were being good friends," I asserted. I still believed that, no matter what he said. I believed his father was trying to do what was best for him. We all watched as he threw his life away, and none of us wanted to see it continue.

He spit, and blood fell to the floor.

Naram stood silently through all of it, and his face dropped. "I didn't give a shit about that position," he said finally. "Your father approached me right after you left and told me it was for the best. You were right about one thing, he didn't think you were fit."

"Shut up," Damyr ground out.

"But once you got back," he continued, "I considered offering you a new trial." My brows rose, this was news to me. "But even once you were back, I knew you weren't better. You were just as weak as everyone thought."

"Shut up!" he screamed. "I am *not* weak."

"Only the weak use underhanded tactics to get what they want because they couldn't get there on their own."

Naram turned away from him, disgust filling his features. "What do we do with him?" he asked.

I glanced at Sorcha, who'd been quietly listening from the back. She added no input, leaving it to us.

"I want him thrown in the dungeon," I demanded. "Prator is already gone. It's over. I want it to be over."

"I'll have my men bring him in."

I nodded, and the three of us headed upstairs. I took Sorcha under my arm as we walked out and away from the building.

It was finally over.

CHAPTER THIRTY-TWO

SORCHA

WE CHECKED TO MAKE sure Damyr was safely locked away before going back to our rooms. Naram went to a pub, and I offered for Zarios to go with him, but he shook his head and told me they needed to process in their own ways.

When we got to his room, we didn't say much, just showering together before drying off and crawling into bed. We were both naked, just savoring the touch of each other.

"Thank you," he whispered. "I couldn't have done any of this without you."

I caressed his face, and he leaned into his touch. "I'm sorry about Damyr."

He brought my hand forward, dropping a kiss to my palm. "It's over now," he said. "He made his choice."

I nodded, staring into his eyes, the eyes I'd learned to read perfectly over the weeks. The eyes that made me feel worthy. "What now?" I whispered.

He kept my gaze, understanding the question. "When this started, I only wished to save my kingdom."

"And now?" I asked with bated breath.

"I would have given it all up if things went sideways. Now, I selfishly wish for both, you and my kingdom. If you feel the same."

I could feel my eyes well. Over the tour, my feelings had shifted. I went into this only wanting a knightship, but as time went on, I realized I wanted more. I wanted Zarios too. I guess that made me selfish as well. "I wished to be a knight, and I still do. I won't be satisfied with just being someone's wife."

He kissed me softly. "If you were, you wouldn't be the woman I fell in love with."

My tears fell freely. "We will figure it out," he continued. "I will do whatever I can to make you happy for all your days. Please, stay."

I smiled, and he wiped my tears. "I will. And I love you too."

This kiss felt final, as if all the pieces of my life were finally falling into place. I felt worthy of my place more than I ever had, and Zarios helped me realize I was all along.

He flipped me on top of him, grabbing my ass and grinding my cunt against his hard cock. I moaned into his mouth, drenched from the feel.

He guided his length inside of me, drawing me down on top of him. I stretched around him, my wetness allowing him to ease in.

His ridge popped in, and the rest of him slid into me until he was seated fully. His hands caressed my thighs as he looked up at me as if I hung the moons in the sky. "Remember your safe word?" he asked.

"Turnip," I recited easily.

"Good girl."

He lifted me and set me back down on his cock with ease. I leaned forward, my hands resting on his chest. I bounced on his cock, savoring the full feeling of him completely inside me. I was sure his cock could be seen through my middle with his size.

He used me, fucked me how he wanted. He would pick up the tempo, slamming into me hard, pulling his ridge in and out of me before slowing down and rotating his hips in the most delicious way.

I drew my tongue to his nipple, unable to sate my curiosity.

I felt his cock twitch, and he groaned under me. I did it again, pulling at it with my teeth.

"Fuck, Princess," he moaned out. I continued playing with him, moving to the other, giving it the same treatment. Seeing him writhe underneath me was satisfying.

He flipped us quickly, bouncing me to the bed and pulling his cock from me as I whined. "Keep doing that, and this will end quicker than I intend."

Zarios worked his way down my body, playing with my nipples, licking every part of me, making me feel alive.

The room was cool, but between the two of us, it felt like a balmy summer day. He pushed my thighs up and stroked my clit with his tongue. "Moons, your tongue," I cursed.

"I'm glad I can please you. I could spend days between your thighs, and it would never be enough."

"Moons, Zarios!" His words brought my orgasm on quickly. Wetness gushed from me, and he licked up every drop, as if he couldn't get enough of my taste.

He kissed down each of my thighs, and I twitched, the sensation sending aftershocks to my pussy.

He easily lined up and drove back into me, filling me in one, quick motion, the piercing on his cock rubbing me in the perfect spot.

His hand snaked down from between my breasts to my lower belly. "You're going to look so hot round with my young," he said. "Everyone will know you're mine."

"Yes," I cried. "Come in me. Claim me."

His hips stuttered as he came deep inside of me. I could feel the warmth pool in my lower belly, and pretending I could be pregnant did give me a rush.

He circled my clit slowly. "I want to feel you come around my cock once more."

I was sensitive, and his slow, gentle circles were exactly what I needed. I ground against him, his half-hard cock hitting me inside. "A bit more," I moaned.

He picked up his pace the smallest amount, and I was coming. It wasn't as intense as the one earlier. No, this one was sweet and pleasant, filling me with a comforting warmth I wished to bask in forever.

Once it subsided, he pulled out and got a washcloth to clean us up. Before he did, he scooped up some of the cum leaking from me and pushed it back in as I let out a small whine.

"I love seeing me inside of you," he confessed before wiping what was left away.

"I kinda love it too." Knowing he painted my insides, made me feel alive, did things to me.

We rolled until he was wrapped around me, my back facing his front. As I drifted off, I felt a bit of cum trickle from me but decided to leave it.

I woke the next morning still wrapped in my fiancée. My *real* fiancé. He was so soft, he felt like the best bedding. I rubbed up and down his chest, my fingers running through his fur. He stirred slightly but stayed mostly asleep. His ear twitched, and I giggled.

His hard length rested against my leg, and I ground my thigh against it.

"Don't stop," he grumbled, still half-asleep.

I took that as permission and snaked down his body under the blankets. His thick cock sat there, hard and red. I licked it once all the way up, playing with the piercing before going to the top and swirling my tongue around it.

I could hear his muffled groans through the blankets as I pushed my hair behind my ears and took him as far as I could in one motion. He was stuffed down my throat, and

I swallowed around him, spending my time tasting him how I wanted.

Suddenly, the covers were thrown up, and I was being moved. When I landed, I was set on his chest, face down, my ass in the air in front of him. "Can't let you have all the fun," he said before licking my asshole.

I took him further down, grinding back against his face. He continued licking until I was soft enough for his tongue to go inside.

It was a feeling I wasn't used to and hadn't experienced, but one I thought I liked. He reached down, gripping my hair and fucking up into me. "Hit me if it's too much," he said before quickly forcing me down.

I let him do what he wanted, sticking my tongue out and letting saliva drip down as he fucked my face hard. Tears stung my eyes, and I coughed for air every time he pulled out.

He continued fucking into me and moved his fingers to my clit, circling it as he shoved his cock down my throat, holding it there. The lack of air mixed with the feeling sent me soaring. I moaned around his huge cock, and he lifted me just as my vision was beginning to darken at the edges. I gasped in giant breaths as my orgasm tore through me.

He shoved me off him and thrusted into my pussy from behind in one brutal movement. He only jerked a few times before he was spilling into me.

We collapsed together. "I can't wait to spend every morning like this."

He kissed my nose. "Me either."

CHAPTER THIRTY-THREE

ZARIOS

AFTER A BRIEF SHOWER and breakfast, there was a knock on the door. "Come in," I called from my seat on the sofa. Sorcha was in the next room, drying her hair.

Kiaza walked in, her clipboard at her side. "Good morning. I hope I'm not interrupting."

"Of course not," I said, though if she had come half an hour earlier, she may have been.

"Great. I wanted to make sure we were all prepared for tomorrow."

My eyes widened. "Tomorrow?" I asked.

She nodded. "The final part of the mating ceremony. It was scheduled for tomorrow night."

My stomach dropped. I'd forgotten all about it. "Cancel it," I said. "I plan on getting rid of that silly practice anyway."

"What silly practice?" Sorcha asked as she walked in.

"Nothing for you to worry about. An outdated mating ritual I'd forgotten all about."

"What is it?" She insisted.

Kiaza looked to me, but she didn't say anything, letting me explain. "As a Grand Clarak, you're expected to show you have the strength to lead by going through an arena match. It isn't to the death, just the last left standing. It's thought that the Grand Clarak's intended should go through a similar physical test to prove themselves."

She didn't have the shocked response I was expecting. "What does it involve?"

"When we've been away, a challenge bracket has been held, now with only two left. They will battle, then the winner will face you. And if they win, they're supposed to be able to petition themselves to me, but in the end, it's my choice. It's ridiculous."

"I'll do it," she said.

I pulled her into me. "You don't have to. You're mine, and I don't care what anyone says."

She raised her brows at me. "You don't think I can win?"

"Of course I do," I said easily. "I just hate it. No one should have to fight in an arena to prove their worth as a spouse."

She shrugged, as if we were talking about the weather. "Well, I guess tomorrow, I do."

I sighed. "You won't let me get you out of this, will you?"

"Nope," she said with a smile. She landed a kiss on my cheek.

"Fine. Kiaza, continue with plans as normal." Though I didn't doubt her, the way I felt about it was true. It was, in the best of terms, archaic. We had moved past things like that a long time ago, but some of those practices remained, like this one. I wanted Valcor to let go of that past and move forward. That was my job as Grand Clarak, and one I took seriously.

"Sounds good," Sorcha said. "I just want a few hours to prepare beforehand."

Kiaza scribbled furiously as Sorcha went back to our room. "Kiaza," I said. She glanced up, her glasses bouncing slightly on her face. "Thank you. For everything. I would be a disaster without you." I knew I didn't say it to her enough. For a moment, I had suspected her during the tour, and I should have known she wouldn't betray me.

She smiled lightly, tucking her things away. "It's no problem, sir. I love my job." She got up to leave but paused at my door. "You know, we do need a new captain of the castle guard."

I followed her gaze, agreeing with her assessment. When she said that, an idea formed. "Could you do me one more favor?" I asked.

I put in my request, and she pulled out her smaller notebook to scribble once more. "I will make it happen," she said before she rushed out the door.

When Sorcha came out a little while later, I all but swallowed my tongue. She was in her full leather practice armor, the same as the first day we met. It hugged her perfectly, and all I could imagine was tearing it off her. Her sword sat on her side, the purple stone in the middle glowing bright.

"You're stunning," I told her.

She rolled her eyes, her hair band hanging from her mouth. "I'm not meant to be stunning. I'm meant to be a warrior." Her words were muffled slightly, only making her cuter.

"You can be both," I said, standing up to meet her. Her hair was neatly tucked in a ponytail behind her. My hands circled her waist, pulling her close. "I love you," I said, just wanting her to hear it. "And the results of this won't matter."

"They matter to me," she said. "But I still love you too. Come on," she said, tapping my shoulder. "You need to help me prepare for tomorrow."

I smiled. "Gladly."

CHAPTER THIRTY-FOUR

SORCHA

WE WALKED HAND-IN-HAND TO the arena. It was a large building at the edge of the castle, made for big events. Zarios told me they used to host fights to the death there often over any silly dispute, but that tradition had long since passed. Now, it was mostly used for performances and any Clarak arena that had to take place.

Even from outside, I could hear the large crowd roar. "Everyone's excited," I said, trying not to let my nerves bleed through.

"Very," he said. "Grand Claraks are meant to claim a mate in the first five years, and I'm the first one to almost push the full five."

"Really?" I asked. "Wouldn't it be when you find someone?"

He shrugged. "It's about producing heirs, I think. Not because they will automatically become Grand Clarak, but because reproduction is seen as a strength."

My nerves came back thinking about that. What if I never wanted to have kids and he was looked down on for it?

"Hey," he said, squeezing my hand through my gloves. "Don't worry about that. We have plenty of time. And if you haven't noticed, I'm not one for sticking to rules."

I smiled and nodded. He was right. We could figure it out—together.

We stepped up to the edge of the arena. I looked out at the dry, dusty ground and the crowd I could see from the other end. "There will be a neutral referee," he told me. "I'm not allowed because I'm on a side. The two opponents chosen to challenge will fight first, and then you will compete against the winner."

"Got it," I said.

"And the ref is there to ensure no one does anything lethal. No magic, no head swings, no attacks if your opponent is already down."

"Sounds like training," I said.

"It is," he affirmed. "But be sure to stay on your guard. The people sent out are usually here on behalf of their parents, and they've been training for this contest for a long time."

"Seriously?" I asked.

"Believe it or not, the few times the intended has been beaten, the Grand Clarak chose the challenger."

My eyes went wide. "Really?"

"Yes. Unfortunately, this kingdom has an obsession with the appearance of power." His words were bitter.

I leaned against him. "Then I better win, huh?" I said, trying to lighten the mood.

He kissed me on the forehead. "I'm going up to the box with the rest of the Claraks." He gestured to where they were. "I'll see you on the other side."

With that, he turned and left. I jumped in place, hyping myself up for what was to come. I was ready. Zarios had been training with me, and I'd been studying up on minotaur fighting styles.

I would win.

An announcer sounded through the stadium. "People of Valcor," they said, their deep voice booming through the space. "It is time for the challenge of the Grand Clarak's intended one."

The crowd roared, and I let it hype me up, bouncing on the balls of my feet. "Let's bring out the current intended, Princess Sorcha Yulean!"

I stepped out, keeping my chin held high. I stood next to the large minotaur who was meant to be the referee.

"And our first challenger, Eshni of the Sperani family." The crowd went wild once again as a deep brown female minotaur emerged. She had a sword in her hand and waved to the crowd.

"And our second Rayon of the Catoryn family." The crowd was even louder this time. She was part gray, part white, with a long braid falling down her back.

"The challengers will face off first, and the winner will face the current intended."

They each sized me up, barely glancing at the other. It made sense. I was just a small human, and ultimately, the one they had to beat. I looked them right back, unafraid of them. To them, I was just a princess, but in reality, I was so much more.

I was escorted back to the edge of the ring to watch while the other two prepared to fight. When the bell rang, they began slowly circling each other. I bounced between them, unsure who I thought would have the upper hand. Rayon was the smaller of the two, but that didn't mean anything.

Eshni swung first, aiming for the left side. Rayon easily blocked, countering with a slash to the middle. It was blocked, but just barely.

The crowd was yelling, excited for the outcome. Eshni went again, this time aiming lower, but she was blocked. This continued on, the opponents trading blow for blow, no one seeming to have the upper hand.

I watched them both, taking in their different techniques. It looked like Eshni was a bit more offensive yet only went for safe moves. While Rayon was more defensive, she struck, she went for harder-to-land moves.

Watching them, they were both very skilled fighters. A match with either would challenge me.

Eshni went for a classic backhand but left her right side fully exposed. Instead of blocking, Rayon went in for the swing. If Eshni would have followed through, she would have hit first, but she changed tactics, trying to block.

Rayon struck her hard. She fell to the ground, and Rayon pointed her sword down to her throat, effectively ending the fight. The crowd went wild, cheering for Rayon.

When the ref called it, Rayon tucked her sword away and helped Eshni up. She took her hand, and they shook, the crowd going wild.

Rayon was definitely a crowd favorite, but when I looked up, Zarios' gaze was firmly on me. He believed in me, and I believed in me.

They took a brief break for Rayon to rest, and I stretched off to the side, replaying the match in my head. I needed to get in early, but I hadn't a clue what I would do.

The announcer came back, telling everyone the next match was up, and I got to my feet.

I could do this.

I walked out into the arena. The sun was beating down, making the back of my neck sweat. Rayon and I met in the middle, and she cut me with a fierce gaze. I had to look up to see her, but that didn't matter. "Here are the rules," the ref said while we both stood. "No lethal moves. No magic, no head shots, no chest stabs. If I see a move I think will cause lethal damage, the match will stop and a winner will be chosen. Understand?"

"Yes," we said in unison.

The referee backed up to give us room. I clenched my sword in my hand, getting into my stance. When the horn rang through the arena, I was ready.

I went for the first move quickly, an easily block-able jab. She did but made no move to counter. "Be careful, wouldn't want to tire yourself too early," she taunted.

I ignored it. I didn't need words. I swung again, a cut to the right. She blocked, but I went for a combo, swiping down to her legs then over to the left in quick succession. She dodged but was a bit thrown from her feet.

This time, she attacked, feinting left then drawing right. I countered, thrusting my sword straight towards her. She had to spin to the side to avoid it. I tried to swing then, but she predicted the move, blocking, even being off balance. Though she needed more than strength to win the match, right now it kept her up where someone of my stature would have most likely been brought down.

She used that force to try and throw me back, but I bore down, holding my ground. The minute I was off balance, it was over. She was just too strong.

Though I wanted to keep pushing her, I had to back off slightly to keep my footing. She righted herself and charged, slashing out of irritation rather than skill. Getting her off balance obviously upset her, and that, I found, would be my in.

I twisted to the side to avoid her and elbowed her in the side as I did. She didn't expect a hand-to-hand move and went to block sloppily, missing entirely. With her back to me, I pressed out and kicked her, hard. It wasn't enough to send her to the ground, but when she turned, I could see her anger got the best of her.

Now, this was just like any other day. Fighting against someone using no tact, only strength.

The crowd buzzed around us, dust kicking up from our every motion, but the only sound in my head was the beating of my heart.

Rayon turned and ran for me, yelling in the process. That was when I knew I found my moment. She tried to undercut me, but like before, instead of going for the block, I went for an offense of my own.

I ducked down and dropped my shoulder just enough to catch her at the knees. She went tumbling over me to the ground, her sword flying from her grasp.

I ran to her, scrambling on top and pressing my sword to the back of her neck. She stopped fighting in defeat, tapping the ground once to signal it was over.

The ref walked over and held my hand up in victory. The crowd roared around us, sending dopamine rushing through me. When I looked up, Zarios, Atalin, Kiaza, and Naram were all on their feet, cheering. When I looked closer, I realized they weren't the only ones.

There, next to them, stood my mothers, Mama jumping up and down screaming, and Mother clapping with a massive smile on her face. Tears welled in my vision. Not once had they come to see me train. It felt as if I proved something not just to myself, but to them.

Rayon brushed herself off and walked over to me, giving me a bow. "You fight well, Sorcha."

"Thank you," I said, my back straight. "You were a worthy opponent."

She scoffed. "Thank you." She walked to the other side of the arena, as did I. When I got out, Zarios and my mothers were waiting for me. I rushed into his arms, and he caught me easily.

I kissed him as if no one was around. "I knew you could do it," he said.

"Me too."

He set me down, and I turned to my mothers. I ran to them, wrapping them both in a hug. "What are you doing here?" I asked.

They pulled away. "Kiaza sent us an invitation," Mama said. "We didn't know at the time that it was a fight, or we may have intervened, but you were amazing out there. We're so proud of you."

"Yes," my mother said. "You've become a fine warrior."

"Thank you," I whispered to both of them. "That's all I've ever wanted to hear."

They smiled down at me.

"Come," Zarios said as I pulled away from them. "A win like this should be celebrated. I know the perfect place."

He led us back inside, my heart full of love.

Chapter Thirty-Five

ZARIOS

We'd spent the evening dining and drinking with Sorcha's parents. They were lovely, despite the war that almost broke out between our kingdoms. It was amazing to see Sorcha come into her own. This fight confirmed something for her, and fuck, she *shone*.

We also all spoke, being honest about the magestone shipments. They admitted the stones were sent earlier, and I informed them we had found the culprit. We didn't tell them about the fake engagement, not wanting to ruin anything going further, but we were all able to come to a peaceful understanding, and more stones were to be sent soon.

About halfway through the night my mother joined us. She had been in the crowd watching Sorcha, and was proud to have her in the family. She continued embarrassing me, sharing stories about my youth, but I heard some interesting ones about Sorcha as payback,

Eventually, we called it a night. My mother went home, her parents retired to their rooms, and us to ours. She was in the shower now, and I finally felt it was time.

The red rope sat on the bed next to me, waiting. My cock throbbed every time I looked at it, imagining her all tied up.

When she stepped out my eyes bugged from my head. She was in a red silk robe that showed off most of her tits and ended right at the tops of her thighs.

"Come here," I said, my voice hoarse.

She padded to me, her full hips swaying. She straddled my lap, and I ran my hands up her body. "What's this?" I asked her.

"I thought you would like it," she said.

"Oh, I do." I ran my finger down the edge against her chest, following the swell of her breast. She gasped, shivering at the touch. "You look marvelous in red."

I pulled the tie holding it to her waist, and it fell away easily. It dropped off her shoulders, exposing her full breasts, all her fair skin. Touching someone without fur all over was odd, but I found I liked the smooth bounce of her skin.

I took her nipple into my mouth, needing to taste her.

She let out a small whimper, leaning into my touch. I pulled away and looked up at her. "Can we try something?"

She nodded. "Anything."

I picked up the rope and started unraveling it. "You know your safe word, right?

"Yup," she said, eyeing the rope. I took the two ends and pulled them around her, twisting it the way I'd seen done.

"Is this too tight?" I asked when necessary. She always said no. It wrapped over her shoulders and around her middle, up between her breasts until I was satisfied. I then used the tie to her robe to bind her hands.

The ropes looked exquisite against her body. "How do you feel?" I asked.

"I'd always liked to be in control," she said. "But allowing myself to let go with you makes me feel...free."

I brought her lips to mine. "Good. I want to be that for you."

I lifted her and brought her to the mirror I had in the corner. I turned her around, holding her hands above her head. "See how sexy you look?" I asked, needing her to see what I saw.

"I see how sexy you are," she sassed.

I landed a hand on her ass, and she yelped. "Seemed you needed a spanking."

I smacked her a few more times, loving the way the sound echoed.

Her ass was left red and sore. I dropped to my knees and kissed the marks, soothing them over with my tongue.

I pushed her forward until she fell against the mirror, catching herself on her forearms. Her tits pressed against the cold mirror. "Don't stop watching, Princess. See what I do to you."

I gripped onto her thighs and spread her open, exposing her to me. Her pussy was dripping wet, her clit engorged. "Look how ready you are for me. I gave you my cock once, and now you can't wait for it again. Can't wait for me to fill you with my cum."

She moaned as I trailed my tongue up her cunt, tasting her musky, sweet scent. She pushed back against me, all but begging me for more.

I was quick to oblige, lapping her up, tasting her in the way I needed. I could see her in the mirror and watched as her lids fluttered closed.

I smacked her ass, and her eyes opened. "Keep watching, Princess. See how pretty you are when you come for me."

She was pretty when she came for me, all flushed with lidded eyes. I was obsessed with her, lost in her body, in her soul.

Her hot breath began to fog up the mirror, though her eyes stayed open. I used my fingers to fuck her, stretching her cunt for me. It was so tight, it wrapped around my fingers, pulling me in. My tongue continued playing with her clit, swirling it around like the best sweet I'd ever consumed.

My fingers bent slightly, searching for that spot that made her melt.

I knew I found it when I felt her channel tighten, her breath catch. I continued rubbing her there.

"Zarios, I'm so close. I'm going to come."

"Come for me, Princess," I said. "Come all over my face."

It only took a few more strokes for her to release, flooding my mouth. I drank it all up, savoring the flavor.

She tasted like mine, and I'd never get over it.

CHAPTER THIRTY-SIX
SORCHA

I RESTED MY HEAD against the mirror, my breathing shaky. The glass was cold, making my already-sensitive nipples tingle. Zarios pulled me from the mirror and brought me to the bed.

He laid me down on my back, standing above me next to the bed. Before, I found it hot, seeing him kneel for me, but this was just as sweet.

"Give me your hands," he said.

I offered them forward, and he took them, bringing them up over my head to the headboard. Right above me was a cut out of a minotaur with horns in the headboard. He hooked my tied hands to the horns, securing me in place.

I tested the hold, wiggling a bit in place, but I wasn't going anywhere. It was high enough that I couldn't move an inch but low enough that I could lay fully on the bed.

Zarios stayed standing over me, rubbing his hand down my body, making goosebumps explode over me. His touch was gentle, skating over the ropes covering my body.

I wasn't lying when I told him that I liked the way it made me feel. I was always in control, always concerned about doing the right thing, but tied up like this, under someone I trusted, I was able to let it all go, able to allow myself to be out of control and reset in a way.

"You're so beautiful," he said, kissing the top of one of my breasts. "And brave," he said, kissing the other. "And all mine." He planted a kiss on my lips.

When he pulled back, he shoved two of his big fingers in my cunt at once, so quickly that I was barely prepared for it.

"Moons, Zarios," I cried out. I tried to wiggle around, but I couldn't move. I was stuck in place.

He soon added another finger, then another, until he had four inside me. I felt stretched so full, and then he bent his fingers up slightly, rubbing against my g-spot with intention.

"Please, Zarios, I need you." I wanted him to fuck me, to take me, to truly make me his.

"You make it so hard to deny you," he said.

His fingers pulled from me, leaving me empty. I needed to be filled. His hand wrapped around his cock as he rubbed it through my cunt, lubing up his tip.

"Do you really want me?" he asked, teasing my entrance.

I moaned, my inner walls contracting with need. "No," I moaned. "I need you."

As I said the words, he sunk into me, making me take him slowly, inch by inch. My back arched, wanting to force him in quicker, but I couldn't move far enough. His movements were slow, torturous, and oh so good. I wriggled again when his ridge popped inside me. I could feel the cold metal of his piercing, only adding to all the sensations.

When he finally bottomed out and I could feel his hips fully sink into me, I felt so full in the best way. Zarios looked at me with reverence, his gaze roaming my body. His hand came up and rubbed between my breasts down towards my belly.

He pressed a spot in my abdomen, and I could feel him rub against where his cock was nestled inside me. A whimper left my lips. It was an odd feeling, like it was moving himself from the outside.

"I can see myself in your tight cunt," he said. "It's so fucking hot."

He pulled out to his tip and sunk back in, snapping his hips once he sank in far enough. His hand resting on that spot, pushing on himself from the outside. He continued that excruciatingly slow pace. This felt different than normal, like my orgasm was building slowly, getting stronger and stronger, but the mild pace made it somehow more intense.

His hands had a hard grip on my sides as he fucked me slowly, with purpose.

"Do you like that, Princess?" he asked.

"Yes," I cried, tears falling from the corners of my eyes. "You feel so fucking good."

"So do you," he began, swirling my clit with his fingers. "I will never get enough of this sweet, tight cunt."

His fingers picked up their pace until I finally let go. This orgasm was much different than any other one I'd had. The slow build grew for so long that when it finally burst, it was the best kind of relief, the kind I wanted to sink into and lose myself in.

But before I could, Zarios was there to ground me, to bring me back.

"Moons, I love you," he said as he began to pick up the pace, his thrusts forcing my orgasm to continue.

I laid back as he fucked into me, used me. It felt like one long, drawn-out orgasm I was floating in, unwilling to leave.

Soon, he lost his rhythm and fucked into me, pushing me into one final orgasm as he fell off that cliff alongside me, pouring his seed deep in my pussy.

Once we both finished, he pulled out, our combined release pooling beneath me.

"That will never not be hot," he said as he took my hands off the hook and began to untie me.

Once I was free and we cleaned up, we laid in bed. I rested my head on his chest, listening to the steady beating of his heart.

"I'm so glad you followed me in the woods that day," Zarios said.

I laughed. "Me too."

His hand rubbed down my back, and I settled in further. "I have something for you," he said.

I sat up. "What is it?"

He reached into his bedside table and pulled out a small black box. When he opened it, I drew a sharp breath. It was a simple gold band with a large ruby sitting right in the middle.

"What's this?" I asked.

"An engagement ring," he said. "My grandmother's. My mother gave it to me when I became Grand Clarak, hoping

I would soon find a mate to settle down with. It took longer than I'm sure she wanted, but I'm glad I waited for you."

Tears welled up in my eyes as I held my hand out. When he slid the ring on, it fell right off. We both looked surprised for a moment before breaking out into laughter. "I think my fingers are a bit smaller than a minotaur's," I said through my giggles.

"So it seems," he said, his deep chuckle warming me. "We can get it resized tomorrow."

"I would like that. Oh! That reminds me." I walked over to my suitcase, taking out the bag with his dagger inside. "It's not sentimental, but I saw it when we went to Mertis and thought of you."

He opened the bag and pulled out the dagger, rolling it in his hand. "I love it," he said. "It's very pretty."

"I'm glad. It's no family ring, but I still hoped you'd like it."

He leaned in and kissed my nose. "I love it, but I'd love anything you gave me."

"That's so sappy," I said jokingly.

He set the dagger and the ring aside and pulled me back into his chest. "You make me sappy," I said. "And I hope you like it, because you'll have to deal with it for the rest of our lives."

I smiled. "I'm sure I'll get used to it."

SORCHA

SIX MONTHS LATER

I sat in my old bedroom, Sage behind me, doing my hair. Sybil was across from me, reviewing paperwork, her hair and makeup already done and her deep green dress on.

"There," Sage said, shoving a final pin in place. It felt like my entire head was made of pins, but when she spun me towards the mirror, I gasped in surprise. My hair was up in a braided bun at the back of my head, intricate curls scattered around to add texture. I had two curls hanging down, framing my face. My makeup wasn't as dark as Sage's, but it gave me some definition and made my lips shiny. I hadn't worn makeup in so long, I'd forgotten what I looked like in it.

"You look like a princess," she said, putting the pins down. She and Sybil were in the same one sleeved dress, but hers was a baby pink.

"I am a princess," I deadpanned.

"Not anymore," Sybil said, joining us. "Now, you're a queen."

"And don't forget captain," Sage added.

I smiled. Right after the mating was declared official, Zarios offered me the job as castle guard captain. At first, I denied it. I was determined to earn my place, I didn't want it just given to me. He was determined that I didn't get it because we were together, but he still allowed me to prove myself to the guards, and they saw my worth as well.

When I first told my mothers, I was worried how they would react. To my surprise, they were nothing but happy for me.

My mama had pulled me aside that day.

"There's something I need to tell you," she said.

"What is it?"

"Your mother isn't the one who wanted to keep you from the knights. It was me."

My brows furrowed in confusion. "I don't understand."

She sighed, dropping her head. "I always wanted what was best for you, and when you showed an interest, I initially thought you would let it go, but you didn't. Your mother thought you could handle it, but the thought of anything happening to you..." A tear rolled down her cheek. "I couldn't handle it. Your mother told me she would take care of it, and I know you think she doesn't support you, but she does. We both do. But she always thought you could do it."

I was stunned. I always thought because my mother was being strict, it was she who wouldn't allow it. I thought it was because I embarrassed her.

"But I am so proud of the woman you've become," Mama said. "And I'm so glad you found your way. I'm sorry I tried to stop you."

"It's okay," I told her, pulling her into a hug. "While I wish things were different, I wouldn't change any of it now."

She gave me a watery smile.

Since that day, my relationship with my mother had improved. We weren't at odds all the time anymore. She didn't even make comments when I wore pants.

My door opened, and my mothers walked in, both looking regal as always. "There you are," Mama said, running to me.

She clasped my hands in hers. "Are you ready?" she asked.

"Ready as ever."

My mother came up next, pulling me into a tight hug. "You look lovely."

I looked at myself in the mirror once more. My dress was a deep maroon, a lightweight skirt with a single slit to look like those in Valcor. The top was an intricate lace with long mesh sleeves.

"We should get moving," Sybil said. "We don't want to be late."

We all headed to the main ballroom, waiting outside the door. The music started, and I watched as Sage walked, then Sybil. My mothers stood one on each side.

The music shifted to a slower, lower tone and the double doors opened. There were what looked like endless rows, all adorned with cascading red and white roses. The aisle was a pretty cream, with petals strewn across it. There were people standing on each side, all eyes on me, but they were all but invisible.

My eyes fell on my husband standing at the end of the aisle. He was in a suit we had to get custom made to fit him. It clung to his body, making him look polished in a way he normally didn't. Though I loved him both ways, this was a nice change.

I stepped in time with the music, moving towards my future, one I was sure would be filled with joy.

When I reached the end, my mothers kissed each of my cheeks before taking their seats.

I stood across from Zarios, my love. Though he had the same hardened look he always did, his eyes shone with light, telling me he was happy too.

We joined hands and listened as the officiant talked of love and life. I hardly heard him, my full focus on the man in front of me.

We repeated our vows, smiling at each other the whole time, meaning every word.

"I love you," I mouthed to him when I was finished.

"I love you too," Zarios mouthed back to me.

I laughed a bit as the officiant gave their closing statements. "Please share your first kiss as a married couple."

Zarios pulled me in, his lips a breath away from mine. "I can't wait to love you forever."

"Me either."

He brought his lips down on mine, and the room erupted in cheers.

When he pulled away, his eyes said it all.

This was no longer pretend.

This was real.

And it was mine.

ACKNOWLEDGEMENTS

I'D LIKE TO THANK my husband, my parents, and my grandmother for always encouraging my career and being my biggest fan. I'd also like to thank my beta readers and my editors Lyonne and Alexa for always making my work shine. And a big thanks to my PA Meg Opalescent, who's helped me take my marketing to the next level. And I wouldn't be sane without my amazing author friends who listen to my crazy plot ideas and help me through the times the plot isn't plotting.

Lastly I'd like to thank you, my reader. Without you I wouldn't be able to do what I do, and I appreciate each and every one of you.

ABOUT THE AUTHOR

LEXIE IS A PARANORMAL romance author and avid reader from Upstate New York. She runs an editing and PA company Morally Gray Author Services and lives with her partner Adi, dog Layla, and cat Swiper. When she's not reading (which is rarely) you can find Lexie playing video games or looking for amazing indie bookstores and vintage shops. Lexie writes campy books full of smut with simp-y monsters looking for love.

Lets Connect!

instagram.com/morally.gray.reads
tiktok.com/@morallygrayreads?lang=en
goodreads.com/author/show/23119761.L_E_Eldridge

Made in the USA
Middletown, DE
15 October 2024

62632018R10166